Dragon in the clouds

Dragon in the clouds

by
Rosemary Nelson

Napoleon Publishing

Cover illustration by June Lawrason

Book and cover design by Pamela Kinney

Published by Napoleon Publishing
A Division of TransMedia Enterprises Inc.

Toronto Ontario Canada

Printed in Canada
02 01 00   9 8 7 6

Canadian Cataloguing in Publication Data

        Nelson, Rosemary, date
          Dragon in the Clouds

        ISBN 0-929141-22-9

        I. Title

        PS8577.E58D73 1994 jC813'.54 C94-931072-7
        PZ7.N35Dr 1994

For Don, Scott and Shaun
my three best friends

The author would like to thank the following for their information and help in the research of this book:

Diane Rakiecki, winner of both gold and silver medals in the Para Olympics in 1984 and 1992, People in Motion, Kelowna, B.C., Kathy Newman, Executive Director of B.C. Wheelchair Sports and Sandra Bennett, volunteer coach for B.C. Wheelchair Sports.

Chapter 1

"Go get it!" I yelled, as I let the frisbee sail out of my hand. Wagner bounded across the lawn after it, his Sheltie tail waving like a white plume. Snapping and growling, he pounced on the frisbee and shook it in his teeth like a rat. Then he raced down onto the lower lawn and around a fencepost where he dropped it.

I must have looked like a better target, sitting in the grass with my legs crossed. Hunching himself into a ball, his tongue hanging out, he hurtled towards me and leapt over my legs. Then he tore around the nearest tree and back. I grabbed him in a head lock, and we wrestled, growling and laughing, until we both became tired of it and lay quietly, our faces close together on the grass.

It was the first day of holidays and my summer stretched out in front of me like a sparkling rainbow. Some kids hate the idea of school ending for two months, but not me! No more piano lessons, no more homework, and no more stopping off at a neighbour's until my parents come home from work. Mom calls it "companionship." She thinks we live too far out in the country for me to be all alone. I call it "being babysat."

Since both Mom and Dad are teachers and have the summer off, I was now going to have lots of time to spend the way I wanted; at the beach, with my friends and with my horse, Ginger.

The best thing of all, though, was the camping trip that my parents were going to take me on. We were going up the Cariboo for two weeks and would be able to go to the Williams Lake Stampede. Mom had said that I could invite a friend. Excitement bubbled up inside me as I thought of all the fun Alisha and I would have sleeping in my pup tent. Little did I know that my mother was about to drop a bombshell into the middle of my plans and blow them all apart!

A hawk's shrill cry sounded high above our alfalfa field as he made lazy circles, looking for his breakfast. I sat up and shaded my eyes against the bright sunlight. Below in the valley, the blue water of Okanagan Lake already shimmered in the heat.

I jumped at the sound of the sliding door as it opened above me on the sun deck. With dismay,

I remembered what I'd been told about staying clean this morning.

"Nikki, come on, it's time to leave or we'll be late for your dental appointment." Mom's voice floated out over the lawn. Then it took on a new tone as she looked down over the railing at me.

"Oh Nikki, look at you! Your white shorts are covered with grass stains and you have dirt smudges on your face. Are those Wagner's paw prints on your blouse?"

At hearing his name mentioned, Wagner opened one eye to peer up at Mom and thumped his tail on the ground. Mom clucked in disapproval.

"Quick, change into your yellow outfit and I'll meet you at the car. Don't forget to throw those clothes in the laundry and comb your hair again." Her voice trailed down after me as I scrambled to my feet and raced inside.

On the way into town, Mom dropped the bombshell!

"Nikki, do you remember your cousin Trevor, from the Prairies?" I could tell by the tone of her voice that she was unsure of how she was going to tell me something.

I looked up at her quickly. "You mean the one that hurt himself on a motorbike and can't walk?"

"Yes, Trevor's been in a wheelchair now for two

years. He's just turned thirteen so he must have been around eleven when it happened. The accident was hard on everybody." She stopped and sighed. "And now, your Uncle Ted and Auntie Mary are going to be getting a divorce."

"Wow, how come?" I breathed. I could hardly remember Uncle Ted, Auntie Mary, or Trevor, even though he was almost the same age as me, but I didn't like the idea of any of my relatives getting a divorce.

Mom glanced at me for a moment, as if she were wondering how much she should tell me. "Sometimes people blame others for the wrong reasons. Auntie Mary blames Uncle Ted for buying Trevor the motorbike in the first place. Even though they've gone for counselling, it's just not working out. And Trevor's causing a few problems at the moment, which isn't helping the situation." She tapped her fingers on the steering wheel and sighed again.

"The reason I'm telling you all this is that Trevor is going to be coming and staying with us for the summer."

My stomach began to feel funny. "He's *what*?"

Mom went on as if she hadn't heard me. "I had a long talk on the phone with Mary last night. She's finding it very hard to cope right now, and she needs some time to sort things out by herself, so...I offered to take Trevor for the summer."

"Great, that's just great," I moaned. I could suddenly see all my plans going down the drain: the days at the beach, the time with my friends, the hours with Ginger, galloping through shadowy forests. Now I was going to have to sit home and entertain a stupid cousin who wouldn't be able to do any of those things.

All at once, another thought struck me. "What about our camping trip?" I wailed.

Mom looked thoughtful for a moment, as if she were suddenly realizing what a big decision she'd made inviting Trevor for the summer. "I don't think we'll be able to manage that now."

I could feel bitter disappointment welling up and pooling in my eyes. Mom glanced at me as she swung into the parking lot. "I'm sorry, Nikki."

I swallowed. It was going to be just like babysitting! What would my friends think!

"He's going to ruin our whole summer," I muttered.

Mom pulled on the emergency brake as we parked under an apple tree outside the dentist's office. She looked at me for a moment. "Nikki, this won't ruin your summer, unless you let it. After all, remember that Trevor is your cousin."

"Yeah? Well, I'm not telling anyone he is." I got out and slammed the door. "When's he coming anyway?"

Mom fixed me with one of her looks. "He's

flying out the day after tomorrow," she said quietly, as she followed me into the dentist's office.

Chapter 2

"Braces!" I shrieked. "I don't care if other kids think they're okay! I won't wear them!" We had just returned from the dentist's office and Mom couldn't understand why I was so upset with the news.

"Of course you'll wear them, dear," she soothed. "You don't want to look like a beaver when you grow up, do you?"

"A beaver!" I stared into the living room mirror. Long, scraggly red hair, blue eyes, a freckled face with a turned up nose...and two large, crooked front teeth stared back at me.

"Who's a beaver?" Dad asked, as he came through the door.

I made a face at him in the mirror. "Mom says I'll look like a beaver if I don't get braces."

Dad chuckled, but said nothing as he walked past me and into the kitchen.

"Summer holidays are supposed to be fun—not full of dumb things like braces and visits from relatives who will spoil everything," I muttered, more to myself than anyone. I stuck my tongue out at my reflection and tried to roll the sides in. I wondered how anyone could do that. My friend Alisha could. She could make neat little tunnels on either side of her tongue. I looked at my teeth. I was wondering what they would look like straight, when I heard Dad tell Mom that he was going up to the Brown's place to see if he could borrow a wrench he needed to fix the car.

I ran into the kitchen. "Can I go with you, Dad, please?"

Dad winked at Mom. "Why, Nikki, of course. I'm always pleased to have your company, but I don't think it's the wrench you're interested in."

Dad was right, although I wasn't about to admit it. The Browns had just moved onto an acreage above us, a few weeks before school had finished, and their son Shawn had joined our grade six class. All the girls had immediately fallen in love with him and were envious that I lived so close to him.

He was very good looking, with curly, dark hair and laughing eyes. He was also the type of kid whom everybody liked as soon as they met him. Even the teachers at my school, including my dad, seemed to enjoy having Shawn around.

"Nice kid, that Brown boy," Dad had said. "He has good manners, too." To Dad, that was the most important thing. It didn't matter what else was wrong with a person. If they had good manners, Dad was impressed.

Shawn had said, "Thank you," to me the second day after his arrival, when his book had fallen off his desk and I had picked it up. It had made me feel good, but I'd become so tongue-tied that I hadn't been able to say anything back.

I wasn't in love with Shawn the way all the other girls were. That's sissy stuff. I thought it would be nice to get to know him though. After all, he was our neighbour. Up until now, I was sure that he didn't know who Nikki Knowles was.

We drove up to the Brown's place, even though it was only a short distance. They lived at the top of a hill behind our house, and my dad wasn't into exercise that much, especially if it meant walking uphill.

Mr. Brown waved to us from the rail fence he and Shawn were working on. Dad got out of the car and headed over towards them. I was about to open my door, when I realized Shawn was coming in the direction of the car. I studied my fingernails as he approached.

"Hi, Nikki."

"Oh, uh...hi," I replied, as I stole a glance at him, and quickly checked my fingernails again. So he did remember my name. I couldn't believe my ears.

"What are you doing?"

"Oh, me? I'm just driving around with my dad today." I suddenly remembered that I hadn't combed my hair. It must look a mess. I grabbed a strand of it and twisted it around a finger.

"What are you doing?" I asked Shawn, before realizing what a dumb question that was. I could see that he was helping his dad and, besides that, I must have sounded like a parrot.

Shawn grinned. "I'm helping my dad put up a rail fence. I want to get a horse this summer."

I stopped twisting my hair. "*You* like horses?" I asked.

Shawn brushed a mosquito away. "Yeah, they're cool. But up till now we've lived in the city and I've never even had the chance to ride one."

"I have a horse," I breathed. "Her name is Ginger."

Shawn grabbed the side mirror and leaned in towards me. "Yeah, I know. She's awesome. I see her in the pasture every time we drive by. Do you suppose I might be able to ride her sometime? Maybe you could teach me a few things."

I took a deep breath and swallowed. Wow!

What would the other girls say if they knew that Shawn had just asked me to teach him to ride?

I saw Dad heading back towards the truck. "Sure," I said quickly. "Do you want to come down tomorrow?"

Locks of curly, dark hair fell over his forehead as he squinted up at his dad, who was lifting a rail into place. "Naw, I'll have to help my dad fence again tomorrow. I could come the day after though."

A happy little shiver ran down my spine. "Okay, see you then," I said, smiling. He smiled back and waved as we drove out of the yard, leaving a blanket of dust hanging in the air behind us.

I was silent on the short drive home. Finally, Dad snapped his fingers in front of me.

"Well, Red, did we get the wrench we wanted?" Whenever Dad wanted to tease me, he called me 'Red'. I didn't really mind though— it made me feel kind of special.

I grinned at him. "Guess what, Dad? I'm going to teach Shawn how to ride Ginger. He's coming up the day after...the day after tomorrow."

"Oh no," I moaned to myself. I had forgotten that was the day my cousin was coming. The awful news about getting braces had pushed the news of Trevor's arrival to the back of my mind. I was just getting to know Shawn. I didn't want Trevor's arrival to ruin that, as well as everything else this summer.

I made a face. At that moment, life seemed very unfair.

Chapter 3

"Nikki, stop grumbling!" We stood in the airport terminal watching the plane glide to a stop. Mom turned and gave me one of her 'cut out the nonsense' looks. "I know you're not happy about this whole thing, and that you'd rather be at home, but it's important that you're here with us to meet Trevor. Now, behave!" She craned her neck to watch as the door of the plane swung open.

I groaned. She was right about that! I wasn't happy about Trevor's arrival. I would rather have been at home. Shawn was coming up in a few hours, and I could have been brushing Ginger, getting her ready to show off to him. Oh, why was all this happening to me?

People streamed past, laughing and greeting others as they walked off the tarmac and through the door. Soon there were no more people. I sighed with relief. He had probably missed his plane and wouldn't be arriving after all.

"There he is," Dad called out. People in front of me were blocking my view. I stood on tiptoes and caught a glimpse of a boy in a funny looking chair being carried down the steps of the airplane by two flight attendants. At the bottom, they lifted him into a wheelchair, and one of them pushed him across the pavement, through the sliding doors and into the throng of people who parted to let them through.

Dad shouted and waved. The boy pointed in our direction, and the smiling flight attendant pushed him towards us.

"Hi, Trevor. How was your trip?" Dad's voice boomed out. The wheelchair stopped in front of us. "Do you remember your Aunt Kay?" He stepped back and waved his arm at me. "And your cousin, Nikki?"

I knew I was staring, but I couldn't stop. Blue-grey eyes. Curly, reddish blonde hair. Freckles. A turned-up nose. I gasped. Trevor could easily pass for my twin...except that everything seemed to come together better on his face...and his front teeth were straight and even. I'd have to admit that he was almost good-looking, but you could tell he wasn't used to smiling, and that kind of spoiled his looks.

He stared back at me, but without a hint of recognition that my face resembled his. Rather, there was something in his eyes that told me I could drop dead any time, for all he cared.

Well, that suited me fine— at least we felt the same way!

He didn't say anything, just sat there with that down-turned mouth. There was a moment of uncomfortable silence. Then I heard my dad's voice again. "Wow, that's some car you have. Where did you get that?"

My eyes slid down to his lap. There was the biggest and brightest red remote-control car that I'd ever seen.

"My mom bought it for me just before I left Saskatoon. It can do lots of things." The words came out in a rush, like he wanted to get them over with. He lifted the car out of his lap and was about to put it over the side of his wheelchair.

"Uh, Trevor, I think you'd better hang onto your car," Dad said. "You may never see it again if you let it go in here." Then he suddenly became aware that I was standing silently at his side. He poked me in the ribs.

"Nikki! You're forgetting your manners. Say hello to Trevor, please."

"Hi, Trevor." I knew my voice held no welcome. I looked at the sullen face and felt my own anger return. What was his problem, anyway? *His* summer wasn't being invaded.

My face must have shown my feelings, as it frequently does. My mother often says I'm wearing my heart on my sleeve. I guess I wear my anger on my sleeve too. Mom's eye caught mine.

She was wearing that 'cut out the nonsense' look again. I guessed I'd better at least pretend.

"Nice...nice car," I stammered. "Where did you get it?"

An audible sigh of relief escaped from Mom. My father stepped behind the wheelchair to push it, but Trevor had already started towards the terminal door. Dad rolled his eyes heavenward. "That's okay, Trevor. Nikki often hangs her ears on the clothesline and forgets them. Let's go home and meet Wagner."

A ghost of a smile shadowed its way across Trevor's face, and he looked at me. I made a face at him, just to show him that he couldn't laugh at me, and that I, for one, didn't appreciate Dad's little joke.

We headed out of the terminal with me trailing slowly along behind. Mom was waiting at the door. Without saying anything, she gave me a quick hug, but I pulled away.

On the ride home, Mom tried to put Trevor at ease by telling him a little about our house. How it has two levels, but because it's built into a hillside, each floor has a door at ground level. Dad had built a small ramp for Trevor's wheelchair at both doors. Trevor's bedroom was in the basement, as was mine. (There's only one bedroom on the main floor and that belongs to my parents.) Because Trevor couldn't use the inside stairs, he would have to go out the front door and down around to the back of the house and in the basement door to get to his room. It would be a bit inconvenient, but we would all help out and she was sure that we'd manage nicely. When Trevor didn't respond to that, she asked him some things about home and how his mother was doing— things she already knew. His answers to her were curt.

When she ran out of things to ask, which didn't take long, Dad took over, talking to Trevor about the Okanagan Valley and about Ogopogo, the famous monster that supposedly lives in our lake.

Most kids my age would probably think that was kind of neat, but Trevor didn't seem to be interested. When Dad found out that he'd never seen a real fruit stand before, he said that we'd stop at the next one we came to. I knew Dad was doing this just to be nice to Trevor, because we buy all our fruit from our neighbours who have their own orchards. I hoped Trevor was appreciating the fact that my father was trying to make him feel welcome, but I doubted it.

I sat as far away from Trevor in the back seat as I could and didn't say anything. I was feeling too miserable to talk. I couldn't stop myself from sneaking glances at Trevor's legs every few minutes. They hadn't moved since Dad had helped him into the back seat beside me. I wondered what it must be like, not to be able to use your legs. I tried not to use mine for a few minutes, but I've always found it hard to sit still. Soon I was swinging my legs back and forth and wiggling my toes again.

Dad swung off the highway and pulled up to a fruit stand, parking the car so that Trevor could see all the different kinds of fruit on display. He and Mom got out of the car. I reached for my door handle.

"We'll only be a minute, Nikki," Mom said. "Stay and keep Trevor company."

I stared out my window at a cat crouching under an apple tree, hungrily watching a bird above him flit from branch to branch. The bird cocked his head and peered down at the cat for a second. Then the twig he was resting on dipped slightly as he thrust against it. Spreading his wings, he soared into the clear, blue sky. How I longed to be that bird!

The silence in the car grew heavy. Did Mom and Dad have to check out every piece of fruit at the stand? I snuck a glance at Trevor to see if he were as bored as I was.

"What are you staring at?" his voice whipped out at me. "Ever since I got here, you've been staring at me!" The freckles on his face stood out in anger and his eyes snapped as he spoke. "What do you think I am, some kind of freak?"

"I have not been staring!" I retorted angrily. "And no, I don't think you're some kind of freak.

You're just rude, that's all."

"You'd be rude too, if your parents sent you away for the summer to some place you didn't want to go."

"Why wouldn't you want to come here? The Okanagan's great!" Then the real reason for my own anger bubbled to the surface. "For your information, Mr. Smarty Pants, I didn't want you to come either. I had all sorts of neat plans made for this summer, and your visit is ruining everything!"

I glowered at him and he glowered back. "Is that so!" he sputtered. His eyes burned into me. "Well, you're ruining my summer too, Witch Face!"

I think I would have hit him, but at that moment Dad opened the car door and climbed in. "Well, have you two made any startling discoveries about one another yet?" he asked in a jovial voice. We both turned and scowled at him in stony silence.

When Mom arrived, Dad began whistling out of tune. He offered Trevor some cherries from the little bag he'd bought, but Trevor said he wasn't hungry. I was too mad to eat, even though cherries are my favourite fruit. I sat staring out of my window, thinking how right I'd been when I decided that my summer was going to be ruined because of Trevor. What a miserable brat he was!

It seemed like a very long ride home. I spent most of it wishing that summer would end quickly.

Chapter 4

I opened the door on the second knock and peered through the screen at Shawn. He was standing on the new ramp my dad had installed at the front door. Behind me in the living room, I could hear Trevor wheeling around. He was probably trying to avoid Mom as she talked to him.

"Oh, uh...hi, Shawn," I stammered. I was about to step outside so I wouldn't have to invite him in, when Mom appeared behind me with a smile of welcome on her face.

"Hi, you must be Shawn Brown." She frowned at me, pushing the door wide open and opening the screen door. "Come on in," she said.

Shawn stepped through the door and wiped his feet. He wiped his feet! Boy, my dad would have been really impressed.

"I'm Mrs. Knowles, Nikki's mother, and this is..." But Shawn had already seen Trevor, who was sitting quietly in the middle of the living room. For once, he forgot his manners.

"I didn't know you had a brother," he blurted out, interrupting my mother.

"I don't have a brother," I said quickly, stepping in front of Trevor. "He's...he's from Saskatchewan." I glanced at Mom, who was imploring me with her eyes to remember my manners. I stepped back again.

"This is...this is my cousin, Trevor. He's going to be staying with us for the summer." I scowled at him as I introduced him. My first impressions of Trevor hadn't changed any.

Shawn was still staring at Trevor. Then he looked at me. "How come he's in a wheelchair?" he asked.

"I was in a dumb motorbike accident two years ago, that's all," Trevor said. He wheeled his chair around and scooped up his shiny red car.

Shawn looked uncomfortable as he suddenly realized that he'd been rude. His eyes slid to the car. "Wow, I've never seen a car like that before!"

Trevor headed for the door.

"Can I...can I watch you work it?" Shawn asked.

Trevor stopped at the door and turned to look at Shawn for a long moment.

"Come on, then. Hold the door for me, will

you?" Shawn glanced at me as he held the door. He was probably thinking what a weird family we all were. I trailed along behind them, not knowing what else to do.

Mom and I watched as Trevor showed Shawn all the moves the car would make. Then, surprisingly enough, he let Shawn use the controls. Soon they were playing a sort of tag. Trevor would use the controls to try to keep the car out of Shawn's reach and then Shawn would take the controls and have the car try to catch Trevor. Boy, could that kid move in his wheelchair! Up and down and around the driveway in circles they went, across the lawn and around the flower bed. Trevor moved fast, darting back and forth, going backwards and pivoting on the spot to change direction.

Wagner thought the game was terrific. Snapping and growling, he chased after the car in a frenzy. Suddenly, it ground to a halt, turned and chased after him. With a surprised yelp, he put his tail between his legs and scurried for safety.

Ginger galloped from across the pasture to watch the action. She reached over the fence as far as she could, flicking her ears and bobbing her head mischievously. Trevor pointed the car towards her. With a huge snort she turned and ran, kicking her legs high in the air.

The game ended when Dad came out to turn

the sprinklers on. He told Shawn and Trevor that it really was unfair to chase the animals and would they please keep the car out of the flower bed, as the petunias did not know how to dodge a red Porsche. Mom brought some milk and cookies out to the lawn where the boys were cooling off under a maple tree.

"Hey, Nikki, want to see the trick I've taught Wagner?" Trevor asked me, as I sauntered over to join them. It was the first time he'd spoken to me since he'd called me 'Witch Face' on the way home from the airport.

I snorted. "You've only been here since this morning. How could you have taught him anything that quickly?"

"I have. Just watch!" he said triumphantly. "Wagner, come here." Wagner jumped up from where he'd been lying chewing a bone and sat in front of the wheelchair.

Just then, my friend Alisha walked in from the road. "What's going on? I could hear all the noise from my place," she said, laughing.

Nothing ever seems to bother Alisha, and she always looks good. That's one of the reasons I hang around with her. I keep hoping some of that stuff will rub off on me. She didn't show any surprise at seeing Trevor in his wheelchair. She just glanced at him and said "Hi". Then she flashed Shawn a smile and looked back to me, waiting for everything to be explained.

Trevor was looking at Alisha all googly-eyed, but when he caught me looking at him, he quickly turned away. I don't think he'd ever seen anything as wonderful. I decided I'd better introduce them, and when I did, his face turned bright pink. He told her about the new trick that he had supposedly taught Wagner, his words all coming out in a rush again.

Alisha laughed with a tinkling sound. "So, let's see the trick," she said.

Wagner was still waiting in front of the wheelchair. I saw Trevor swallow and take a deep breath.

"Sing, Wagner, sing!" he commanded. And, amazingly enough, Wagner did sing. Well, sort of. With a couple of high pitched yelps, and a low throaty growl to get him going, he slowly tilted his head backwards, opened his mouth and emitted a long "Aa..ow..hhhhh". He was concentrating so hard that his front paws bounced up and down off the ground as he tipped his head back.

Shawn and Alisha collapsed with laughter. Wagner, satisfied that he'd done a good job, leapt up onto Trevor's lap, wagging his tail and wiggling his behind. At the same time, he slathered his tongue all over Trevor's face.

"Not bad," I admitted begrudgingly, though, inside me, something stung. After all, Wagner was my dog. I was the one who should be teaching him new tricks.

I jumped up and brushed off the dust and grass on my shorts. "Come on, Shawn, let's go ride Ginger. You guys can watch if you want," I said, as I headed to the garage where I kept the saddle and bridle.

Alisha straddled the rail fence while I showed Shawn how to put the saddle on. I knew from listening to Dad that the best way to teach people is to have them do things themselves. Trevor sat near the fence all hunched over, with his remote control car on his knee. Wagner leaned against the wheelchair and watched everything, his tongue hanging out. He still looked pretty proud of himself for the singing he'd done.

Ginger was usually a quiet horse, but today she was a bit spooky. She kept eyeing the car on Trevor's lap and snorting at it as if she expected it to leap up at her at any moment.

Finally, we were ready. "Okay, I'll get on first and just show you a few things," I said, as I grabbed the reins in my left hand.

Alisha looked good, and most boys are taken in by looks, but I really knew how to ride. I figured Shawn would be impressed with that, since he wanted to learn himself. Some day, I would have to show him the ribbons I'd won barrel racing in local gymkhanas.

I jumped up onto the first railing of the fence. Ginger was too high for me to reach from the ground, and she was usually patient enough to allow me to lean over her until I could get my left foot into the stirrup and hoist myself over.

Today, though, she was jittery. Just as I got my left foot into the stirrup, she nervously stepped away. I quickly tried to throw my weight over her back, and as I did so, I felt the saddle begin to slip off sideways. Too late, I realized that I'd forgotten to tell Shawn that you always retighten a saddle before you get on a horse, because most horses blow up their tummy when they're being saddled.

I somehow managed to scramble up onto her back, but the saddle continued to slide. Before I knew it, I was sitting on her back on top of the girth, and the saddle was swinging wildly under her belly.

With a crazed snort, and one look at the red car, Ginger took off across the pasture, bucking to try and free herself of the despicable growth on her stomach.

The reins flew out of my hand and I clawed at her mane for something to hang onto. I managed to last through two bucks, but on the third one, as her head went down, she twisted sideways. My grip was lost. She kicked high into the air and I sailed off, landing headfirst a few feet away.

I sat up quickly and shook my head to clear

the stars. The saddle had finally worked its way off completely. It lay upside down in a heap, while nearby, Ginger munched calmly on some grass.

Shawn and Alisha arrived breathless at my side. Trevor still sat on the other side of the fence, his mouth gaping open. Wagner lay beside him, nose between his paws, whining.

"Scaredy-cat dog! Stupid horse!" I muttered to myself, as I slowly got up.

"Are you okay?" Shawn asked, looking at me in disbelief. Then I could see the laughter in his eyes, and the way he was having a hard time keeping his mouth straight. I felt something wet on my cheek and wiped the back of my hand across it, smearing it over the rest of my face.

Alisha stepped daintily over a thistle that I'd narrowly missed landing on. "Phew! What's that awful smell?" She leaned towards me. "Nikki, you've got horse manure all over your face." She wrinkled her nose in disgust. "Ooo...you look terrible. Look, you've even torn your shorts." And then, almost as an afterthought, "Did you hurt yourself?"

"No, I don't think so," I said angrily, as I limped towards the house. It would take a few minutes before I knew myself if I were hurt.

As I crawled through the fence past Trevor, he chuckled. I glared at him.

"Nice face," he commented.

"Oh yeah?" I sneered. "Well, it's all your fault. You and that stupid car! Let's see how it looks on you!" I scooped some of the gooey mess off my face and plopped it on top of his head. Then I quickly walked away and left him muttering words I couldn't hear.

"Shawn," my mom's voice called out from the door. "Your mom's on the phone. She wants you to go in town with her right now." She walked outside to see if we'd heard her. She stopped short when she saw me.

"Nikki, for goodness sakes," she gasped. ""What happened to you?" After checking me over from an arm's length, she decided I was okay.

"Get Alisha to use the garden hose and wash you off, dear. You can't come in the house to shower until all that horrible horse manure is off you."

At this point, Shawn said his good-byes. He was probably relieved to have an excuse to get away. Alisha giggled as she and Trevor took turns drenching me with the garden hose, the horse manure splattering off in every direction. Finally, I had to laugh too, but not before I'd asked Dad if he'd go out and take that "stupid bridle off that stupid horse".

I left Alisha and Trevor having a water fight and headed in for a shower. I checked myself over carefully in the mirror. A few scratches were all I could see. Though no doubt a few bruises would show up tomorrow, I was able to admit to myself that probably the biggest bruise was to my own ego. As I climbed into the shower, I imagined that Shawn was up at his house, laughing at me, at that very moment.

Chapter 5

"Hey, open your mouth and let's have a look," Alisha said to me. It was a week or so later and I'd just arrived home with my mouth full of metal.

"No way," I moaned, holding my hand up in front of my mouth. "They look awful."

"You do look a little like 'Jaws', but other than that, they're not so bad," Trevor said.

I looked behind Alisha to where Trevor sat. That kid was still really bugging me. I've got to admit we hadn't had to look after him the way I'd expected we would. He could do a lot of things without help, such as dress himself, get in and out of bed and use the bathroom. Mom said it had been a lot of hard work on Trevor's part to learn all of those things since the accident.

I begrudgingly had to agree— but it still bugged me that he was going to spoil our whole summer. Mom and Dad were spending a lot of time fussing over him, and he didn't seem to appreciate it one bit. He still hardly ever smiled, and every time we were near each other for long, we'd end up in some sort of a fight. He seemed to have a real chip on his shoulder.

In spite of all that, he had started to follow me around a lot. Shawn hadn't been back for a visit, so Trevor always wanted me to play with that dumb car. Sometimes I did, just to get rid of him for a while.

Whenever Alisha came to visit, he stuck to us like glue. I knew he really liked Alisha. She wasn't nasty to him the way I could be. When she was around, we usually just tried to ignore him and pretend he wasn't there. But today, his remark about 'Jaws' made me angry.

"Get lost, Trevor," I said. "Come on, Alisha, let's go to my room." I tried not to notice the hurt look in his eyes, as we stepped past him and left.

Once we were in my room with the door closed, Alisha eyed my new braces critically. "Trevor's right. They're not so bad."

"Yeah, not so bad," I muttered. "He also said I look like 'Jaws'." I made a face. "What a disgusting brat he can be sometimes."

"Oh, he's just teasing," Alisha said, as she

watched me gaze woefully at myself in the mirror. "Remember, other people have them too."

"Yeah, who?"

Alisha put her finger on her chin thoughtfully for a minute. "Well, there's John Brooks."

"Yuk, that creep! Now I suppose people will make a pair of us just because we both wear braces," I moaned.

"And there's Miss Dawson," Alisha went on.

"Miss Dawson!" I exclaimed. Miss Dawson had been a new teacher at our school last year, and, believe it or not, she'd had braces. But she must have been at least twenty-five. "She's old. That doesn't count."

Alisha giggled and plunked herself on my bed. "Well, just think, in two years, your teeth will be straight and you'll be beautiful," she said.

"Two years!" I groaned, "I'll be going into grade nine! I need a new look now." I held a handful of my red hair up in my fist and glanced at Alisha in the mirror. "Do you think Shawn would like my hair if it were short?" I asked.

Alisha was silent for a moment and looked uncomfortable. Then she caught me watching her in the mirror. "Maybe," she said, with a smile.

I hadn't had my hair cut for nearly three years. I pulled a long strand of hair up and let it slide slowly through my fingers. Yes, I would do it! Now that I'd made the decision, I couldn't wait for any old hairdresser.

I ran upstairs to the main bathroom and yanked open the drawer of the vanity. All I could see was a pair of nail scissors. I grabbed them and headed for the kitchen drawer where the big scissors were.

By the time I got back to the bathroom, I'd made another decision. I rooted around in Mom's make-up bag, trying to decide what to take. I knew what all the stuff was for, but I'd never had much interest in it before. Finally, I just grabbed the whole bag. She and Dad were out for the afternoon and by the time they got home, I'd be all done with the experimenting and everything would be put back.

Alisha gasped as I kicked the door of my room shut with my foot and laid everything on top of the junk already on my dresser. She jumped off the bed. "Nikki, you're not going to.... Oh Nikki..." Her voice trailed off.

I'd already held a long strand of my hair out to the side and chopped it with the big kitchen scissors. It came off a bit shorter than I'd expected, and now I was going to have to try and do the same all over my head.

A few minutes later, long strands of red hair lay in a fan around my feet. I inspected my cropped head in the mirror and whirled around to face

Alisha, who'd been watching me, speechless.

"Well, what do you think?" I asked her. I thought it didn't look too bad. It was a bit uneven, and I'd really done a job over one ear, but that would grow back.

"I think you've just invented a new hair style." Alisha began to giggle, then laugh. Finally, she threw herself on the bed in an uncontrollable fit and laughed until the tears ran down her face.

I snorted. It didn't look that funny. I shook my head and ran my fingers through what was left of my hair, then looked in the mirror again. I did look radically different. I began to get the giggles too and dove onto the bed beside Alisha in a fit of laughter.

I finally sat up and looked at Alisha. "You know," I said, "what I'd really like is blonde hair like yours."

"Mine?" Alisha squeaked. I couldn't tell if she was pretending to be surprised or not.

"Yeah, yours," I said. "Everybody likes blondes, don't they?" I remembered something my mother had used on her hair a while back to bring out gold highlights. At the time, I thought it was silly— now it didn't seem to be.

I found it in the back of the cupboard in the bathroom. Alisha and I read the directions carefully. It didn't seem so hard to use. You just sprayed it on, combed it through, and then used a hair dryer on it. The heat from the hair dryer activated the lightener which gave the hair wonderful golden tones. There were three applications in the bottle. Mom had used one. If I used both of the others at once, it just might turn my bright red hair into gold.

This time, Alisha helped. We sprayed and combed and sprayed and combed until my head was saturated with the stuff. Then we decided it was too wet to use the hair dryer on right away, so while we let it dry a bit, Alisha and I applied the make-up.

Some beige liquid, when smeared on thickly enough, covered most of my freckles. However, it seemed to make me look awfully pale and pasty-faced. So on top of that, we brushed lots of rose-coloured blusher.

Next came the eyes. We decided on green eyeshadow, blue mascara, and a line of blue eyeliner around the whole eye. Alisha did one eye, and I did the other. Since neither of us had an experienced hand, and both of us had a different idea of what the perfect eye should look like, the final effect was somewhat startling. However, it seemed passable. A coral pink lipstick was the final touch.

"Hurry, let's get the hair done. I've got to go soon," Alisha said, as we studied the new face in the mirror. "I can't wait to see how this turned out," she continued, as she grabbed the hair dryer. We found out only too soon. As the heat dried my hair, it began to turn, not gold as we had anticipated, but a light, sickly red colour.

"Well..." Alisha said thoughtfully, as she laid the hair dryer down, "that's not exactly what we expected." She skipped over to the window. "Come over and see if the sunlight brings out any gold."

I dreamily floated towards the window with a smile on my face. I had a vision of myself with clouds of golden hair forming a halo around my face.

Alisha gasped. "Oh, my gosh!" she exclaimed in horror. "What's the matter?" I squealed, as I grabbed the hand mirror and looked at my reflection.

It was green! In the sunlight, my hair was green! I looked at Alisha in dismay and could see that she was on the verge of another laughing attack. It was fine for her to laugh. She had the golden curls—I had the green ones. Curls! I'd never had curls before. I looked again. Cutting my long hair had made it go curly, and I kind of liked it.

We decided to wash my hair, hoping that some of the colour would come out. However, the colour had already come out. Washing and trying it a second time only made it a shade lighter. It also shone more brightly green in the sunlight.

Finally, Alisha had to go. After she left, I wandered around looking in mirrors for a few minutes. I definitely had a new look all right. If I stayed out of the sunlight and didn't open my mouth so that my braces showed, I thought I looked quite passable.

So this was the way grown-ups felt. I found myself upstairs looking in Mom's closet and running my fingers along her things. My hand stopped at an electric blue dress that was one of my favourites. I slipped it off the hanger and over my head. The full skirt billowed out and floated slowly down to my ankles. I cinched the belt around my waist and pirouetted in front of the mirror. I looked at the top of the dress and sighed. There was a lot of room to be filled there. This year, I'd have to talk Mom into letting me at least wear a training bra.

I spied a pair of white high heels in the closet and slipped them on. I'd tried them on when she'd bought them, but now they fit! Wow!

I peeked out of the window. Trevor was below on the backyard lawn, throwing the frisbee for Wagner, who was happily retrieving it over and over again. His car sat not too far away. No one else was around. I just had to show someone this new me. I secretly wished Shawn were here, but he wasn't, so Trevor would have to do.

I tottered downstairs holding the handrail for support. My feet hurt already, and I wondered how it were possible to wear these things all day. At the doorway, I hesitated, took a deep breath and swallowed. Then I stepped out into the sunlight.

Chapter 6

Trevor wheeled around at the sound of the door opening, and Wagner sank down on his haunches beside him. Both of them looked at me for what seemed like an eternity. Then the frisbee fell to the lawn, and Trevor's mouth dropped open. Wagner let out a questioning whine and pressed himself closer to Trevor's legs.

"Nikki?" Trevor croaked. "What happened to your face?" He gasped. "Your hair...it's green!" A smile began at the corner of his mouth and spread across his face. Then with a hoot, my cousin, who supposedly didn't know how to, laughed and laughed and laughed. Every few seconds, he'd gasp for air and take another look at me. Then he'd start again, until finally there were tears rolling down his cheeks.

Wagner just sat cocking his head from side to side and looking at me. Something in my appearance must have triggered vague recognition, but he just couldn't seem to figure out who I was.

Heat began to rise from my neck up into my face. I stood for a moment, trembling with rage, uncertain what to do. Then I spied a pitcher of ice water sitting on the picnic table. That would cool Trevor's laughter.

I leapt onto the lawn, only to have my high heels sink into the grass and remain there while I tried to take another step. I pitched forward onto the grass, leaving both shoes neatly stuck behind me.

This made Trevor laugh even harder. Wagner was enjoying it too. He leapt up on Trevor's knee and began licking his face.

I pulled myself up off the ground, grabbed the ice water and dumped it on top of Trevor.

His howls of laughter stopped. He was soaking wet, choking and spluttering. But my revenge was still not complete. I grabbed the transmitter to his remote control car from the grass. I was going to send that car down the hill as fast as it would go until it ran out of energy. Then let Trevor try to get it back! I didn't care if he ever saw that dumb old red car again.

I grasped the box in both hands, pulled the antennae out and started the car on its downward journey. Trevor must have known what I had in mind. He started towards me.

You could tell by the look on his face that he was mad!

Just then, I saw a car coming up the hill. It was Mom and Dad! With a shriek, I dropped the transmitter and ran to retrieve Mom's high heels which were still stuck in the lawn. With a backwards glance at Trevor, who was wheeling over towards the transmitter, his face like thunder, I raced towards the basement door.

I had just enough time to get into the bathroom and lock the door before I heard the car doors slam and Mom and Dad walk by, just outside the window.

"Trevor, how come you're all wet?" my mother exclaimed, and then, as if she intuitively knew that I had something to do with it, she asked, "Where's Nikki?"

I held my breath and waited for Trevor to rat on me. When he did, I was going to be dead! I was about to open the door and own up to everything when I heard him say, "Aw, we were just fooling around...I don't know where she is now."

I couldn't believe my ears. Why hadn't Trevor taken the opportunity to tell on me? I heard the door open and the rustle of grocery bags.

"That Nikki!" my mom muttered to my dad, as they headed up the stairs. Intrigued by what promised to be an interesting conversation, I listened until they walked down the hall and into the kitchen, and then I quietly went upstairs.

"Yes, I know what you mean," Dad said, as he started putting the groceries away. "She's either ignoring Trevor or she's fighting with him."

The water started running, which probably meant that Mom was making a salad for supper. "It's not helping Trevor's confidence, which is already low. Missing that year of school didn't help either."

Standing in the hallway out of sight, I frowned to myself. I hadn't noticed that Trevor lacked self-confidence, and I hadn't known that he was behind at school either. The truth was, I didn't know much about Trevor at all, except that he was an unlikeable brat most of the time, and that he'd spoiled a lot of my plans for the summer.

I became lost in thought for a few moments, until I heard my dad say, "Hand me the Kleenex and I'll put it in the hall closet."

I ducked back down the hallway and into the bathroom. I stepped behind the door and held my breath as Dad opened the hall closet next to the bathroom, rummaged around and found a place for the Kleenex. I heard him walk back to the kitchen.

Somehow I was going to have to get out of this get-up...and fast. I stepped out from behind the door and, in doing so, caught sight of a weird-looking person in the bathroom mirror. I let out a startled yelp, before I realized that it was my own reflection I was looking at.

"What was that?" I heard Dad say. I quietly closed and locked the door. My heart hammered in my chest. Now what was I going to do!

"Nikki, is that you?" My dad was right outside the door. I held my breath hoping that he would go away, but he must have known that I was doing something I shouldn't be. I once asked my mother how it is that parents always know these things. She told me that a little birdie tells them. Ha!

"Nikki, open this door right this minute," my dad thundered.

There was no use waiting any longer. With a sigh, I opened the door and watched the expression on my father's face change from anger to shock.

Unfortunately, at that moment, my mother appeared around the corner with the salad she'd been making. She took one look at me, threw her hands in the air, and screamed. As the tomatoes, lettuce and salad bowl battled with gravity and lost, Mom stood and gaped at me.

"Nikki?" she finally squeaked.

I had some fast talking to do to get out of this one.

Chapter 7

I lay back in the soft grass, cushioning my head with one arm and enjoying the sunshine on my face, which was now scrubbed clean of make-up. Trevor and I were in my favourite area of our yard— a grassy spot surrounded by trees at the end of the driveway. I'd done some thinking about what I'd overheard Mom and Dad talking about and decided that it wouldn't hurt me to spend a bit more time with Trevor. After all, he hadn't finked when he'd had a chance to cause lots of trouble for me. Maybe he wasn't as bad as he always seemed to be.

"Was she really mad?" He wanted to know all of the details about what had happened when I'd been discovered in the bathroom.

I plucked a piece of grass and began chewing on it. "Naw, she wasn't too mad. She was a bit ticked off that I'd used her stuff without asking, but she finally ended up laughing about the way I looked. She made an appointment for tomorrow so I can have my hair trimmed properly—and to see what can be done about the colour."

"What did your dad say?"

I pursed my lips indignantly. "He told me the next time I put make-up on, to have one person do both eyes. He said that I was the closest thing to an alien he'd ever seen."

Trevor hooted. "You looked almost as funny as when you fell in the horse manure. Too bad Shawn wasn't here. He would have thought you were hilarious!" He looked at me and snorted. "You sure do some stupid things."

"Me! Well, you're not so clever yourself you know." I was sorry as soon as the words came out of my mouth. I remembered what Mom had said about Trevor being behind a year in school and about his lack of self-confidence. The comment I'd just made wasn't going to help things.

I could tell from the look in his eyes that I'd hurt his feelings, but he wasn't about to let on. "What do you mean?" he sneered.

"Well, I don't mean you're stupid. I just mean...I just mean you're hard to be around. You seem to have a chip on your shoulder all the time."

Trevor scowled, and I could tell that that subject was closed. I waited silently for a moment, wondering what we could possibly talk about that wouldn't end up with us in a fight.

"Have you written your mom yet?" I finally asked.

Trevor looked out across the field. "No, not yet...but I will this week." He stopped and the silence became heavy. I knew that Trevor had something more he wanted to say. Finally, he looked at me. "You're sure lucky to have parents who get along," he said.

I'd never given much thought to my parents' relationship. Now I considered it. I nodded my head. "Yeah, I guess so."

"My parents split up because of me," Trevor went on.

I sat up, confused. "Because of you! What do you mean?"

"Ever since my dumb accident they've been fighting about whose fault it was, and really, it was my own fault. I was going too fast. If it had never happened, they'd still be together."

"Oh, wow," I breathed. "You've been worrying about that all this time." I watched a butterfly flit through the air and land on the branch of a nearby tree. "I hardly remember Aunt Mary or Uncle Ted," I said, "but if they really cared about each other, I don't think your accident would have made any difference." I looked at Trevor. "It's not your fault that your parents separated."

Trevor sighed, and I could tell that he would have liked to believe me, but I guess the guilt he'd been feeling had been with him too long. He shook a lock of curly hair out of his eyes and stared into the distance, his jaw set in a hard line. He didn't say anything.

I took the chance to ask him about something that had been on my mind since I'd overheard Mom and Dad talking. "I heard Mom say that you're behind a year in school," I said quickly.

Trevor lowered his eyes and looked at his lap. "Yeah, after the accident, I spent a lot of time in the hospital. I had to have a lot of physiotherapy and stuff, and when I finally got back to school, I was way behind in reading and math, so last year they made me repeat grade five."

"Couldn't you have caught up with a tutor to help you?" I asked.

"Naw. My parents couldn't have afforded a tutor. Besides, I'm not that good at school anyway."

I chewed on my grass and, for once, said nothing more. White clouds drifted lazily overhead.

"Look! I see an old man," I said.

Trevor leaned forward. "Where?" he demanded.

"Up there, in the clouds." I pointed over my head to the shape that I thought resembled an old man. Trevor looked at me as if I were crazy.

"Don't you ever pick shapes out of clouds?" I asked.

Trevor shook his head. "No. What would I

want to look up at clouds for, anyway? My neck gets sore enough just looking up at people all the time."

"Well, you have to try it." I locked the wheel of his chair and got him to grab onto me so I could help him get on to the ground. Soon we were lying side by side watching for shapes to form in the fluffy white clouds overhead.

I showed Trevor my old man, which was rapidly changing into a cat. Before long, he was discovering all sorts of things by himself, and I closed my eyes to rest them for a few minutes.

I was awakened suddenly by Trevor's excited voice. "Nikki, look! Look at the dragon." I gazed over to the east where he was pointing. There, hanging over the lake, was a magnificent dragon. With folded wings and an open mouth belching clouds of fire, it sat on giant, toe nailed feet; a long serpent-like tail coiled around its body.

We lay mesmerized by what our imagination was doing with this giant cloud. As the wind tore along high above us, it nibbled at the cloud's edges and changed its form. Now the tail straightened out and the feet disappeared. The mouth opened wider in fury as the giant wings unfolded for flight.Then it was an elongated dragon with wings and neck outstretched, soaring through its sapphire kingdom. Finally, it was nothing but a long cloud scurrying along in the air currents high above us.

"Nikki." Trevor's voice was quiet. "If you could have one wish, what would it be?" he asked me.

I sat up and thought for a moment. "That's easy. I'd like to have nice straight teeth without these stupid braces," I said. "What would your wish be?" I helped him struggle his way back into the wheelchair. I was pretty sure I knew what his wish would be.

"I'd like to be that dragon in the clouds," Trevor said dreamily, staring up at the sky.

"The dragon in the clouds? Why?" I asked, somewhat confused.

"Did you see how powerful he was, and how he could change into anything he wanted to be?" Trevor's voice caught, and he said no more. I had the feeling that he was finally reaching way down inside himself and dealing with some feelings that had been bottled up for a long time.

I was thoughtful as we headed back towards the house. When we came out of the trees, Wagner came charging over and leapt onto Trevor's lap.

"You know, I bet if Dad were to tutor you over the summer he could help you catch up in school. They might even let you go into grade seven in the fall," I said, patting Wagner on the head.

"Naw, I'm too far behind. Besides, your dad has enough to do this summer without helping me." I could tell from the tone of his voice that our conversation was over. He pushed Wagner off and we went into the house silently, each of us lost in our own thoughts.

Chapter 8

"Hey, that's not bad," I shouted over to Shawn, as he cantered Ginger around the last of the three barrels that I'd set up in a triangle in the pasture. He'd been coming down every day for the last week to ride. I hadn't had to do much teaching— he was just kind of a natural with horses, and he'd learned quickly. His dad had told him that maybe next week they'd put an ad in the paper for a horse. Soon we would be able to go riding together.

"What did Shawn say about your new look?" Alisha asked, as she hung over the fence with me, watching Shawn. She'd been away on holidays with her parents all week and this was the first time I'd seen her since the day I'd cut my hair. The next day I'd had my hair reshaped, and then rinsed with a special stuff to tone down the green. The hairdresser said that she'd never seen such a mess in her life, and she hoped that I wasn't considering going into hairdressing when I grew up.

"He liked it," I answered, telling a little white lie. Shawn hadn't exactly said that. In fact, he hadn't said anything at all. His mouth had just dropped open a bit when he first saw me. He hadn't commented on my braces either. I took that to mean my new look was okay.

"I'm going to a show with Shawn tomorrow night," Alisha said, watching me out of the corner of her eye.

"*You* have a date with Shawn?" I asked.

Alisha tossed her head, her hair falling back over her shoulders. "No, I don't, silly. Mrs. Brown phoned and asked me if I'd like to go with them— we're all going. That's not much of a date, if you ask me."

I snorted. "It's close enough! Besides, I thought you and I were going shopping tomorrow night. I've already asked Dad about driving us in."

Alisha's face began to change colour. "Oh, I forgot about that," she murmured.

"Never mind," I said, in a tone that I couldn't disguise. I turned away from her, not really understanding why I was acting that way. Trevor was making his way over to us. He must have just discovered that Alisha was here.

"Nikki, are you mad at me because I'm going to the show with Shawn?" Alisha asked quickly. "You told me before school was out that you weren't interested in boys, especially Shawn."

"I'm not," I retorted, "and no, I'm not mad at you." I turned back to the fence and put my chin on my folded arms.

"Hi, Shawn. Hi, Alisha," Trevor's voice said from behind us. Alisha turned with a smile on her face to greet Trevor. That's one thing I've got to say about Alisha, she was friendly to everyone, not just Shawn.

Shawn pulled Ginger to a stop in front of us. "That's cool. I can hardly wait until next week when I have my own horse," he said, as he slid off the saddle.

I crawled between the rails and took the reins from him. "I'll show you how it's done in a real race," I said, ignoring Alisha as I stepped up onto the rail and jumped onto Ginger's back.

She wasn't used to me being rough with her, and I guess I was still feeling a bit hurt and angry, although I'd just told Alisha I wasn't.

"Haw!" I yelled, as I wheeled her around and kicked her in the sides. At the same time, I slapped her on the rear end with the reins. We took off like an arrow!

Usually Ginger listens to me when we race, but today she ran like a wild thing and turned around the first barrel so tightly that she overturned it. Kicking great clods of turf in the air, we headed across the field for the second one. By this time, she was in a hard gallop, and it took all the strength I had in my arms to get her to make a big circle around the barrel. Then we were off to the third one. There was no turning her this time. We raced past it and kept straight on going.

I yanked on the reins and shouted "Whoa", but she was so excited, she didn't even hear me. She finally stopped when she came to the fence at the top of the pasture. We stayed up there until she had calmed down.

As we turned and trotted back towards the kids, I could see they were laughing at me. Why did I always have to do such dumb things when Shawn was around?

"So that's how it's really done in a race," Shawn said grinning, as I rode up. Then, he must have noticed the look on my face. "Just kidding," he said, glancing at Alisha. She shrugged her shoulders.

Trevor must also have seen the way I looked. "Come on, Shawn, let's go shoot some baskets," he said. "I'll have you a game of '21'. Come on Alisha."

I unsaddled Ginger and brushed her as I watched the three of them over by the garage.

Dad said that Trevor had been good at sports before the accident. We'd moved the basketball hoop down a bit to make it easier for him. I watched as he shot his fourth basket in a row.

Since Shawn had been spending quite a bit of time at our place lately, he and Trevor were becoming friends. It meant that I didn't always have to be playing with Trevor and his car, but whenever Shawn was with him, I usually tagged along anyway. Trevor and I hadn't fought as much this past week, ever since our talk. I don't know why, but there just didn't seem to be as much to fight about.

I put the tack away in the garage and went inside to get a snack. I was beginning to feel ashamed of the way I had acted. I knew that I had no real reason to be mad at Alisha or Shawn.

"Hey, Trevor," Shawn said, as they came over to the lawn where I was sitting munching potato chips, "you'll have to get Nikki's mom to drive you up some night for a sleep-over. Maybe we could sleep in the tent or something."

Trevor's face split into a grin. "Really? Wow, that would be great!" It seemed to mean so much to him that I was pretty sure he hadn't slept over at a friend's house in a long time. I wondered if he even had any close friends at home in Saskatchewan.

"I'll bet she'd drive me up tomorrow night if I

asked her," Trevor suggested, still beaming.

Shawn glanced at Alisha. "Oh, I can't tomorrow night. I'm...I'm going out."

"You couldn't anyway, Trevor," I blurted without thinking. "You and I are going to the show tomorrow night."

"We are?" Trevor asked.

At the same moment, Alisha and Shawn looked from Trevor to me and said, "You are?"

I had clearly caught them all by surprise. I tossed my head. "Yes, we are," I said.

Chapter 9

Unfortunately, when I'd made my plans so hastily, I had forgotten to consult Mom and Dad.

"I'm sorry, Nikki, but your dad and I have a meeting to go to tonight for a couple of hours, and it's in the opposite direction." She must have seen the disappointed look on my face. "I think tomorrow night would be all right."

"Nikki, you amaze me," Dad said, as he handed me the jam and syrup for the breakfast table. "A few weeks ago, you swore that Trevor was going to ruin your entire summer. Now you want to take him to a movie."

"Well, after all, he is my cousin, you know," I said, sitting down at the table.

"I'm just teasing you, Red. I think it's great. Yes, I'll take you in town tomorrow night and...why don't we all go to the beach this afternoon? Phone up Alisha and Shawn and see if they want to come too."

I had a vision of Shawn and Alisha googly-eyeing each other at the beach all day. I didn't really want to watch that. "Naw," I said, frowning, "let's just make this a family affair today."

Mom and Dad glanced at each other, and I decided to change the subject quickly. Trevor wasn't up yet, and this seemed a good time to ask Dad about something that had been on my mind.

I pushed a piece of pancake into a puddle of syrup and watched it become all soggy. "Dad, would it be possible for you to tutor Trevor and help him catch up in school?" I asked, all in one breath.

Dad's piece of pancake halted in midair on its way to his mouth. "Well, of course, I'd help him...if he wanted help." He laid his fork down on his plate and leaned forward. "I don't think you know this, Nikki, but that was one of the main problems with Trevor at home. He didn't want a tutor."

"He didn't?" I asked, in disbelief. "He told me that his parents couldn't afford a tutor."

"Well, it wouldn't have been easy, but they could have managed. Trevor refused, however, and so, after some counselling, the school decided to leave him where he felt most successful."

"Oh, wow," I breathed. "Well, he's not stupid, and I think he could catch up."

Dad got up from the table with his dishes. "Nikki, I know he's not stupid, and I think he could perhaps catch up, but, before it will work, Trevor's got to make up his mind that he can do it." He gave my mom a quick kiss as she walked by him into the kitchen and then he went outside.

I sat and ate my breakfast silently for a few minutes, deep in thought. Now it was time for *my* pancake to halt halfway to my mouth. "Mom, do you think that twelve years old is too young to date?"

I popped the pancake into my mouth as I heard some dishes clatter into the sink. Mom's head appeared around the door. "Date!" she exclaimed. "Whom do you want to date?"

I chewed dreamily. "Not me, Mom! I'm just asking.... Well, do you think twelve is too young?"

Mom cleared her throat. I could tell she was unsure of the purpose of this conversation and where it was leading her. "Well, yes, it is pretty young." Then she took a firmer stand just in case the opinion referred to me in any way. "Yes, it's definitely too young." Her face took on a faraway look. "Why, I was nearly sixteen when I had my first date."

I stabbed my last piece of pancake. "Oh, Mom, that was a century ago. Things have changed."

"Nikki, it was not a century ago! I'll have you know that I'm only thirty-four."

I rolled my eyes. That seemed like a century to me. "Well, it just so happens, I also think twelve is too young." I collected my dishes and got up from the table. "Do you know what? Alisha is going to the movies tonight with Shawn."

There was a moment of silence. "Hm...m...m," was all she said.

"They're going with Shawn's mom and dad," I added.

Mom smiled. "Nikki, I would hardly call that a date."

"Well, it's close enough to a date for me, and I think they're too young!" I headed for the door.

"Nikki," Mom called after me. I stopped and looked back at her. I could tell she wanted to laugh. "Would you have felt that twelve was too young, if it had been you going to the show with the Browns instead of Alisha?"

"Very funny, Mom!" I said. I let the screen door slam shut behind me as an exclamation mark.

Chapter 10

It turned out to be a hot, sultry day and I was glad we had come to the lake. Mom and Dad lay on the beach reading, while Trevor and I fooled around in the water for most of the afternoon. Trevor knew how to swim, but because his legs couldn't help him and he tired very easily, he wore a life jacket.

I threw a rubber ball to Trevor, and, as he caught it, I noticed that he had a pretty good build. He'd developed big muscles in his arms and shoulders because he'd had to use them so much.

I wondered if Alisha would have liked him for a boyfriend if he hadn't been in a wheelchair. Perhaps Trevor also wondered a lot about "What if..." Maybe that's why he always seemed to have a chip on his shoulder.

I dove under the water as I saw the ball coming at my head. There was no use any of us wondering "What if..." because Trevor was never going to walk again. But that didn't mean that he couldn't do lots of other things, like catch up in school. I just had to convince him that he could do it.

It looked like we were in for a storm as we drove home just before dinner. Dark clouds were gathering in the west, and every few minutes, thunder rumbled far off in the distance.

Mom ran in to make a quick meal before she and Dad left for their meeting, and I went and moved Ginger from the pasture to her corral so she wouldn't overeat.

"We won't be long, dear," Mom said, as they were leaving. She hung on to her skirt as the wind whipped at it. A streak of lightning—much closer now—lit up the sky. "You'd better put Wagner in the house, Nikki. You know how frightened he is of thunderstorms."

With Wagner cowering safely under the bed—a trick he always pulled during a thunderstorm—and Trevor writing a letter to his mom, I decided to bake some cookies. I'd baked quite a bit and I was pretty sure that Mom wouldn't mind me doing it when she wasn't home. I found the recipe for oatmeal cookies and turned on the oven to 350 degrees. Then I collected the ingredients and started mixing them together. I had one pan almost ready for the oven when Trevor called me.

"Nikki, how do you spell Ogopogo?" he asked,

as I walked into the dining room. At that moment, the whole place lit up with a flash of lightning and a deafening crash shook the house.

"Wow, that was close," I said, more to myself than to Trevor. I didn't usually mind thunderstorms. In fact, I found that feeling of a certain energy in the air exciting, but I didn't like it when thunder dropped on top of the house as it just had.

I glanced over Trevor's shoulder as I spelled Ogopogo for him. The letter was a disaster, and I wondered how his mother was ever going to be able to read it.

"You're sure a rotten speller," I said, without thinking.

Trevor slammed his hand down over the letter and leaned over it so I couldn't see it. His face turned all red.

"So, nobody asked you!" he yelled.

"Yeah, you did. You asked me how to spell Ogopogo. Okay, okay, don't get so excited. I just mean, you need a lot of help with your spelling and your capitals and stuff."

Trevor continued to glare at me. "And what if I don't want any help?" he muttered.

"You know," I went on, "I bet I could help you." I suddenly had a vision of myself up in front of a blackboard with a long metre stick, pointing to words. I was elegantly dressed in high heels and a blue dress, and I had very long bright, red fingernails. Twenty-five children sat attentively in front of me, their faces shining in anticipation of the lesson. Why, I was probably cut out to be a teacher, and this would be excellent training. "In fact, if I got Shawn and Alisha to help..." I went on.

"Alisha! No way!" Trevor shouted. "I don't want her to know how stupid I am."

I threw up my hands. "You are not stupid. You just act stupid sometimes." I stalked into the kitchen, threw the rest of the dough in little balls onto the second sheet and then squashed them with a fork. Then I carefully opened the oven door and pushed both pans in. After setting the timer for ten minutes, I went back into the livingroom, just as another streak of lightning flooded the sky.

Trevor was still labouring over his letter, probably spelling every second word wrong and forgetting all his capitals, but too proud to ask for help.

A sudden gust of warm wind whistled through the screen door and lifted a pile of papers off the buffet. They fluttered and swooped around the room like captive birds. I ran to close the door.

I heard Wagner whine behind me. It was surprising that he was out from under the bed, because the thunderstorm was still raging outside. He ran past me and pushed his nose against the screen door, sniffing.

And then I smelled it. Smoke!

I pushed open the screen door and ran outside. I stared in the direction of our alfalfa field and the forest behind it, mesmerized by the sight of thin tendrils of smoke which, in between hot gusts of wind, twisted upwards from the trees like insidious snakes. At the same time, I could hear an ominous crackling. My heart lurched wildly.

Forest fire!

Chapter 11

I could see flames beginning to leap into the air from the trees, even though it was some distance away. The fire was being fanned by the wind and would soon be racing in every direction.

I turned and looked at Trevor sitting at the table, a curly lock of hair falling into his eyes. The line of his mouth was etched in frustration from trying to write the letter to his mom. He was concentrating so hard on finishing it, that he hadn't even noticed the smell of smoke.

That's when I panicked. I could run and probably get down to the highway if there were no one home at Alisha's. But Trevor couldn't. Suddenly, without my beckoning it, something inside my chest squeezed painfully hard. I took a couple of deep breaths. I had to get him out of here! But how?

I heard Ginger whinny nervously. She had probably smelled the smoke and was frightened. Without saying anything to Trevor, I ran out the door and past Mom's car. Hot wind blasted me in the face, sucking my breath away. Lightning sizzled through the air and seemed to play tag with me as I scrambled across the pasture with Wagner on my heels.

I fumbled with the latch on the corral until it opened and Ginger rushed past me in a flurry of flying hooves. My reassuring words to her were swept away in the wind. Then I turned and ran back towards the house, leaving the pasture gate yawning open behind me. That's all I could do for her. I prayed that she would have enough sense to get out.

While I'd been doing this, my mind had been a jumble of tumbling thoughts. What was I going to do about Trevor? I ran past Mom's car and then stopped and spun around, eying the car with sudden inspiration. I chewed on my lip and hesitated. I didn't know how to drive, but...I was somehow going to have to drive it! I yanked the car door open and found her keys on the dash. My heart pounded in fear at the thought of what I was about to try and do, but one glance up at the fire told me that I didn't have any other choice.

I ran to the screen door and took a deep breath to try and calm myself. "Trevor, come on. There's a forest fire. We've got to get out of here. Did you hear me? There's a forest fire!" I tried not to shout, but my voice was becoming hysterical, and the words came out louder than I'd intended them to.

Trevor looked up from his letter, and the colour left his face as he gazed through the screen door at the burning forest. He didn't move.

"Quick!" I shouted. I pushed the door open and held it for him. "Come on to the car. I'll help you get in."

Trevor wheeled down the ramp and over to the car. "Who's going to drive?" he asked in a daze.

"I am," I said, a little more confidently than I felt.

"*You!* Uh uh, no way I'm going down that hill with you driving." The determination in Trevor's voice was strong.

"Look, Trevor, you've got a choice," I yelled. "You either get in the car with me, or you probably end up like a piece of fried bacon in the middle of that fire."

"I'm probably dead either way," Trevor muttered. He must have caught the look on my face as I opened the car door. "Okay, okay, I'll come with you. How am I going to get in?"

I put my hands under his arms and tried to lift him out of his wheelchair, but no matter how hard I tried, I just didn't have the strength. He probably weighed more than I did. I finally straightened up, puffing and panting, my back hurting. Wagner whined beside us, but I ignored him.

I quickly tried to think of what else would work. "Move your chair in as close to the door as you can," I suggested, "then maybe you can pull yourself up by using the doorframe, and I can help you in."

Trevor rolled his chair in tightly against the open door, as I had asked, and stretched his arms up. He caught hold of the top of the doorframe and stopped for a moment to catch his breath. Then he shut his eyes and pulled. Struggling, he slowly drew himself out of the chair.

"Hang on", I said, as I tried to pull the chair out of the way. It got caught in some gravel and didn't want to move.

"Hurry up, will ya? I can't hang here all day," Trevor grumbled.

"I am hurrying," I muttered, too tired to think of anything more clever to say. "Okay, I'm going to swing your legs in. Hang on tight!" As I lifted his legs into the car, he suddenly let go of the doorframe. I pushed him as hard as I could to make sure he fell into the car, and when he did, I fell in on top of him!

"Whew! We made it," I exclaimed as I scrambled

across him and crawled into the driver's seat. Wagner didn't wait to be invited. He leapt onto Trevor's lap, tail between his legs, and shoved his nose under Trevor's arm to hide his head.

"Do up your seat belt," I shouted, as I jammed the key in the ignition.

"Ha! Are you kidding? It's already done up," Trevor shouted back.

I turned the key on and the car leapt forward as if a crazed animal were under the hood. Then it jolted to a stop.

Trevor braced his arms against the dash. "Take it easy, will you! Don't you know how to use a clutch?" he hollered. Wagner jumped off Trevor's lap and cowered on the floor.

"What's a clutch?" I snapped back. I just wanted to get out of there fast. I glanced over at the fire which seemed to have moved a lot closer. If it reached the trees which separated Shawn's place and ours, it would follow the tree line right down to our house. The way the wind was whipping around, it wouldn't take long!

"The clutch is that floor pedal on your left," Trevor said, as he pointed down at my feet. "The right one is your brake."

"I know what a brake is," I muttered.

"Do you know how to shift gears?"

My head was swimming. "Shift gears? No..." I threw my hands up in despair, bowing my head. I clenched my eyes shut and tried to stop the tears from rolling down my face. I'd failed. I wasn't going to be able to get us out after all.

Trevor's hand touched mine. "Nikki, don't cry. Look, I know what to do. I'll tell you. I can also shift the gears."

My mouth opened in awe. "How do you know about all that?"

Trevor shook it off with a pleased grin. "Aw, prairie kids always learn how to drive when they're young. My dad was teaching me when...when I got hurt." I looked at him in a daze. "Now, get us out of here. Drive!"

And drive I did. With Trevor telling me what do, we lurched and bumped along the driveway, narrowly avoiding an apple tree, and turned onto the road leading down to Alisha's.

Since Alisha's, Shawn's, and my family are the only ones living on our road, I didn't have to worry about traffic. What I did have to worry about though, was how fast the car wanted to go downhill.

"Nikki, use your brake!" Trevor hollered. His face was white as he watched the bushes rushing past.

I slammed my foot on the brake. The car swerved and jolted to a stop, pitching us both forward. Wagner whined and began to scratch at the door.

As we sat there, trying to get up enough nerve to start the car again, there was an earsplitting crash of thunder, and moments later, big globs of rain started hitting the windshield. Then it came down in sheets. I fumbled for the windshield wipers.

There was another rumbling sound overhead, faint at first. Then it grew stronger. I peered out the window at the sky. "Look, Trevor, it's a water bomber! Someone's reported the fire. Hooray!" I squealed, all in one breath.

I started the car again, with one foot on the brake and one on the clutch, as Trevor told me to. Then I let my foot slowly off the clutch pedal, and we jerkily started down the hill again.

When we turned into Alisha's driveway, I went weak with relief. Her parents were standing at the window watching the water bomber head for the fire through the rain. When they saw my Mom's car drive in, they ran to the door.

Trevor shifted into neutral, and I quickly switched the ignition off. "I'll run in and explain things. Alisha's dad can come out and get you," I said, jumping out of the car into the pouring rain.

I ran up the steps as the door opened wide. "Nikki!" they both exclaimed at once. I saw them glance over my head at the car and both their mouths dropped open.

I smiled proudly. "I had to drive it down. I had to get Trevor away from the fire."

"Your car, it's rolling away!" Alisha's dad shouted.

I whirled around to see Trevor's terrified face pressed against the window as the car rolled backward, gathering speed.

"Nikki!" I heard Trevor's voice wail, as the car rambled down the grassy slope of lawn. There was a dull grinding sound as it ran over a lilac bush and a muffled thud as it came to rest against the fence.

At that moment, my mom and dad went racing past on the road. I saw Mom glance into the yard, and, a couple of seconds later, there was the sudden screech of tires.

"Oh, no," I moaned, covering my face with my hands. Gentle arms enfolded me and led me, dripping wet into the house. Alisha's mom hugged me and sat me down on a kitchen chair. Then she went to open the door for Mom and Dad. Alisha's dad was right behind them, carrying Trevor. Even Wagner, soaking wet, got to come in.

"I had to get Trevor away from the fire," I wailed, and then I burst into hysterical tears. Perhaps if I cried, Dad wouldn't be so mad about the car.

It worked. "It's okay, Nikki. You did the right thing," Dad said, hugging me tightly.

"I knew that Shawn's parents weren't home, and I didn't know if Alisha's mom and dad were or not. I just had to get him out safely," I continued to babble. "I was busy baking when..." My voice faded away, and I gasped.

"Nikki! Your cookies!" Trevor croaked. "You didn't turn the oven off."

"Quick, into the car everyone," Dad said, as he headed toward the door. "We may have a fire of our own to put out."

Chapter 12

My shoulders ached from standing so long in one spot at the sink, scrubbing. By the time we'd reached the house last night, smoke was seeping out of the oven door, and the cookies had been nothing but puddles of black char. The house still stank from the combination of burned cookies and the pungent odour of wet, burned wood from the forest fire. For the last half hour, I'd been scraping and scouring cookie pans, and I was ready to swear they'd never come clean.

"What a mess," Mom mused, as she stood by the screen door, drinking her coffee and watching the scene up back. The forestry people had come out to make sure that there were no hot spots left and to assess the damage from the fire. Dad was over talking to them.

I shook my hands free of water and joined Mom for a moment, glancing over her shoulder. I felt sick as I stared up at the blackened remains of what only yesterday had been an area of beautiful green trees. The fire had burned part of our pasture too, and had just been starting into the line of trees that separated the Brown's place from ours when it was stopped.

"We were lucky, Mom," I said, and I shuddered as I thought again of last night and how frightening the whole thing had been.

Mom turned and brushed past me to go in to the kitchen. There were tears in her eyes. She hardly ever cried! I looked away quickly so that my eyes wouldn't fill up too.

"Nikki, please don't ever bake again unless we're here," she said gruffly. I sighed and returned to the sink. I was not about to argue with her at this point.

"Aunt Kay, are you in here?" Trevor's excited voice hollered from the doorway. Once again, I trailed to the doorway behind Mom.

Shawn stood behind Trevor's chair. They were chattering away together like two magpies. I watched Shawn for a moment. He didn't look any different, but then I guess one date wouldn't make a person look too much different.

"Oh, hi, Nikki..." Shawn looked a bit uncomfortable when he saw me. "Some excitement around here last night, eh? How come you were home? I thought you were going to a show."

Now it was my turn to be uncomfortable. "Well, we were...but we didn't," I finished lamely.

"Nikki, get back to the kitchen. You're dripping soapy water," Mom scolded.

As I returned to the kitchen, I heard Shawn ask my mom if Trevor could stay overnight at their place. They planned on sleeping in Shawn's tent in the front yard. Mom must have said yes, because a few minutes later I heard her rummaging around in the basement closet, looking for a sleeping bag.

I was sick of cleaning cookie sheets. I squirted a bunch of detergent on them and left them in a sink full of water to soak. I dried my hands and went down to the basement.

"Nikki, did you hear? I'm staying over at Shawn's tonight. We're sleeping in his tent." Trevor's voice bombarded me as soon as I appeared.

"Here, I think this one will do, Trevor," said my mom, backing out of the closet with a cobweb stuck to her hair and eyebrow. She brushed a hand across and pulled it away, making a face. Then she laughed. "You can tell how long it's been since we've used this stuff. I guess we should go camping more often."

The angry retort about missing the Cariboo trip that I would have given a few weeks ago didn't materialize. It didn't seem quite as important any more.

"Why couldn't we go camping for just a few days somewhere around here?" I asked.

Mom looked at me thoughtfully for a moment and then at Trevor. "That might be a good idea, Nikki. We'll see how Trevor makes out tonight, and then we'll talk about it."

She rolled the sleeping bag up. "I want to make a batch of jam and then I can drive you up to Shawn's," she said to Trevor.

"If it's okay with you, I'd like to go back up with Shawn now. I'll push myself up."

Mom frowned. "It will be hard for you. It's a fairly steep hill."

"I can push him if he gets tired, Mrs. Knowles," Shawn said. "We want to set up the tent and..."

"I won't need help," Trevor's voice cut in sharply. "If I get tired, I'll stop and rest." Then he made a macho face and flexed his arm muscles. "I'm strong you know. Look at this!"

Mom laughed. "Okay, you win. Go ahead. I'll drive your stuff up later. Just make sure you leave out what you want me to bring," she hollered after them as they raced to the door.

She turned to me. "And you, young lady, can return to the cookie pans and finish them."

"How did you know I left them? I suppose it was that little bird again, telling you things," I grumbled.

Mom grinned. "Yes, a little bird in the water pipes. I heard you filling the sink up. Now, come on, I'll need all of the kitchen in a few minutes when I get my jam underway."

I slowly followed her upstairs and finished the despicable job, deciding then and there that I had baked my last batch of cookies, ever! Then I hung around and watched Mom make the raspberry jam so that I would be able to lick out all the pots.

Soon I found myself sitting at the dining room table looking out the window, idly kicking my legs back and forth. I got up and sat down on the couch with a book, but I only read a page before I put it down. The house seemed strangely empty.

I wandered from room to room, looking for something to do. I even went downstairs and opened the door to my room, thinking that I might want to clean it. But one glance inside, at junk piled everywhere and an unmade bed, made me close the door again.

Then I meandered into the spare bedroom which Trevor was using. It was almost as much of a disaster as mine, but he didn't have as much stuff as I did, and his was spread around at a lower level. The bedspread had been pulled up in haste to cover the crumpled sheets underneath, and on top of the lumps sat the things Mom was to take to Shawn's later. The table beside the bed was littered, and a few things lay scattered around on the floor. The top of his dresser, which he found difficult to reach, had nothing on it except a piece of paper.

I walked over and glanced at it. It was the letter he'd been writing to his mom the night before. If it had been all folded up, I wouldn't have touched it. Even I know that's bad manners. But it was lying face up and I couldn't resist reading it.

Dere Mum,

im having a good sumer altho i mis you and dad. my car stil works and nikki and i pla with it alot. the okanogan is a grate place did you kno ther is a monster named Ogopogo that livs here in the lake. it is fun to be staying with a rele family. Nikki was a pain in the but when i first got here now she just fites with me once in a while. she is teaching me to read...

I frowned and reread the last sentence. What a fibber! He had refused my help when I had offered, although maybe deep down that's what he really wanted. Well, now that I'd seen that letter, he was going to get my help whether he liked it or not. I just had to figure out a way of approaching the whole thing.

Still bored, I headed down to Alisha's with Wagner at my side. I wanted to find out how her date with Shawn had been.

"It wasn't a date, I told you before!" Alisha said to me as we huffed and puffed our way back up the hill towards Shawn's house a few minutes later. We had decided we would see if the boys had the tent up yet.

"Did he kiss you?" I demanded. I had no idea how fast one progressed in dating, but the idea of kissing was somehow terrifyingly exciting. The question sent Alisha into spasms of laughter. She continued laughing the rest of the way up the hill, and we arrived hot and out of breath.

"Nikki!" Shawn's voice yelled at me, as we rounded the corner and came into view. "I've been trying to phone you. Guess what! I have a horse! Dad's just brought her home." The grin on his face stretched from ear to ear.

Behind him on the lawn, Trevor was bending over from his chair, struggling to pound in a tent peg. He looked excited too, but you could tell that his mind was more on sleeping in a tent than on the arrival of a horse.

"Wow, I see her. She's cool. What's her name?" I asked, looking over to where a white horse watched us from the corral.

"Her name is Star. Come on, let's go see her," he offered and set off in a lope, with me close behind.

Star eyed us suspiciously as we climbed up on the railing of the corral. When Shawn stuck his hand out towards her, she snorted and tossed her head. But it was a snort that seemed to say, "I'd kind of like to get to know you, and if you'd have brought me an apple, I'd be right over." We both laughed.

"When can you ride her?" I asked eagerly.

"Dad says to let her settle in until tomorrow. Maybe you could come up and go riding with me in a couple of days."

"Sure," I replied happily. I was aware of Alisha and Trevor coming up behind us, and I turned to say something to them.

"The tack came with her too. Come on, I'll show you. It's in the barn." Shawn set off again with me in tow, leaving Alisha and Trevor. I looked over my shoulder and saw Alisha saying something to Trevor, and then they headed back towards the house.

I felt a pang of guilt. This had started out to be Trevor's big day. By the time we got back to the house, however, I could see that Trevor wasn't upset. He and Alisha had finished putting the tent up, and Trevor sat in front of it, beaming as if he had just climbed Mt. Everest.

I peered inside the tent. "So, you guys aren't

afraid of the bears, eh?"

"Bears!" they both exclaimed together.

"I bet there aren't any bears around here," Trevor said.

"Yes, there are," I retorted smugly. "I've seen their droppings when I've been riding."

"Well, I'm going to be too excited to sleep anyway, so I'll hear them," Trevor replied confidently.

"Remember, you're not supposed to have food in the tent, either. Bears have a terrific sense of smell," I added.

"Oh, Nikki, stop being such a know-it-all," Alisha cut in. "You're just trying to scare the guys."

Her words stung. I turned and glared at her. "I am not."

Shawn quickly changed the subject. "Speaking of food, I'm hungry. It must be lunch time." He glanced at his watch. "Come on, Trevor, let's go make a sandwich. He looked over his shoulder at us. "You guys want to stay?"

I glanced at Alisha and she shook her head. I guessed she was still a bit angry with me. "No, we've got to get going. We'll see you tomorrow."

"Have fun, Trevor," Alisha hollered, as we walked out of the driveway.

She was quiet for most of the way home. I acted silly, hoping to fill the silence. Sometimes when I feel good I get giddy, and I make up silly poetry.

"Here we go loopty loop
Here we go loopty lie,
Here we go loopty loop
Just like a bird in the sky," I sang. I stretched my arms out in the warm sunshine and soared and swooped down the road. Then I stopped and waited for Alisha to catch up.

"Here we go loopty loop
Here we go loopty lie,
Here we go loopty loop
Just like a worm in the apple pie." I dove into the ditch beside the road. I was about to become a worm— anything to get Alisha smiling again.

"I think he likes you, Nikki," she suddenly said. I scrambled out of the ditch, ignoring the grass stains on my knees.

"He what? Who?" I asked, as I fell into step with her again.

"Shawn. I think he likes you." She made a face. "He spent most of last night telling me about the new horse he was getting and how he'd be riding with you." She kicked at a pebble and then smiled at me. "Besides, I don't even really like horses."

I stopped and looked at her. "You mean, you don't like him any more?"

Alisha put her arms into the air and stretched

on her tiptoes for a moment. Then she frowned. "I like him, but I don't think I want him for a boyfriend or anything like that."

It was my turn to be silent. I wasn't sure I wanted him for a boyfriend! But it thrilled me to think that he liked me. Whether or not it was because of the horses, I didn't care at that moment.

I turned to Alisha to find her smiling at me. A grin worked its way across my face. I put up my hand, palm facing her. "Friends?" I asked.

She slapped her hand against mine. "Friends," she said.

Chapter 13

I unzipped the zipper on our tent and crawled inside on my hands and knees, a potato chip bag hanging from my mouth, a handful of comic books in one hand and a flashlight in the other.

"Phew, I think that's the last trip I have to make," I said, collapsing onto my sleeping bag. There was a whine behind me, and Wagner stuck his head through the flap.

"Come on, Wagner, there's just enough room for you," Alisha said, as he crawled in on his belly. She zipped up the flap behind him.

After coming home, Alisha and I had decided it would be fun to have a sleep-over too. Both of our parents had agreed, so earlier in the evening we'd put up my own pup tent down on the lower lawn. Then we'd filled it with all the necessities: sleeping bags, air mattresses, an extra blanket for each of us in case it got cold, a jug of lemonade and two glasses, insect repellent, a suitcase with my clothes in it for tomorrow, my slippers, some books, and my toothbrush and toothpaste. I wanted to be like a real camper in the morning and be able to get all ready in the tent. I had my ghetto blaster too, but the batteries were dead, and I couldn't find an extension cord that was long enough to stretch from the house to the tent. I shoved it into a corner by my feet.

I heard Mom and Dad coming to say, "Good night". They peered through the screening. "It looks like we'll see you in a few days, Red," Dad said, with a smile on his face.

"Very funny, Dad. We're just well prepared, that's all. Besides, we're practising so you'll take us camping next week."

Dad looked at Mom. "Yes, dear," she said, "I thought if Trevor makes out all right, we could go down to one of the Provincial Parks on the lake for a couple of nights next week."

"It sounds fine to me," he said, "but I'm not so sure that Nikki will have pulled up stakes here by then." He smiled again and they both blew us a kiss and left. A few minutes later, the darkness began to sift down over our tent.

We rearranged everything to try and give us more room— everything that is, except Wagner. He didn't want to be rearranged. The air mattress was doing funny things to him and he was scared to move. When we put our weight near him, it

94

would go down. Then when we moved away—boing! It would pop up again, Wagner with it. Finally he must have decided that it was a game. When my back was turned, he suddenly leapt upon me, his tail wagging furiously in Alisha's face. He began licking me on the nose and mouth.

I turned and grabbed him around the middle. Then I rolled over onto my back, holding him to my tummy with his legs in the air. He thrashed his tail and legs about, struggling to get free, while I rolled back and forth, growling in his ear. Finally, with a burst of energy, he wriggled free.

Normally, this sends him into a frenzy, scuttling around the yard in circles, as fast as he can run, but inside the tent there was no place to go. He hurtled into one of the nylon walls, and then turned and leapt across my back to pounce on top of Alisha. Giggling, she dove into her pillow head first. Soon the tent walls were moving back and forth as we tried unsuccessfully to subdue Wagner.

Suddenly, the end pole got kicked over and, as that end began to collapse, the other end pole silently toppled too. The tent drifted down on top of us like a soft parachute, and we had to wiggle our way out like cats from under a blanket.

We lay in the grass gulping in air which was fragrant with the smell of freshly mown hay. A silver dollar moon was just peeking over the mountains, throwing shafts of light onto the water of Okanagan Lake far below us. I watched the darkened house for a moment, half expecting Mom and Dad to have heard us, but no lights came on. Wagner lay, panting, beside us. I found the flashlight and, a few minutes later, we had the tent back up. This time, we put the ghetto blaster, my suitcase and the extra blankets outside the door.

I stretched out in my sleeping bag and reached for the bag of potato chips, ripping off the end and offering some to Alisha. She gasped. "Nikki, you told the boys to make sure there was no food in the tent!"

I snorted. "There are no bears around here, silly."

"But you said you've seen their droppings."

"I have," I insisted, "but that's up back in the woods. I've never seen any in our yard."

The three of us munched on potato chips for a few minutes without talking. I took another handful, held them against my mouth and then ate towards them. Crumbs flew in every direction.

"Let's go scare the boys," I said, as the thought suddenly occurred to me. "We'll pretend to be a bear!"

Alisha flicked on her flashlight. "Are you nuts? It's dark out there." She looked at her watch. "Besides, it's 11:39."

"Don't be a chicken. It's not so dark," I said, unzipping the tent flap and poking my head out. "We can easily see in the moonlight, and we'll take the flashlight. Come on." I crawled out and pulled on my jeans, then my runners.

Alisha appeared behind me, yawning. She looked like she would rather have been going to sleep. Wagner, however, bounced out, ready for an adventure.

"Sorry, Wagner, you have to stay here." I opened the door to the garage and pushed him inside. "We'll be back in a few minutes," I whispered to him, as he whined from the other side. I hoped he wouldn't bark.

The cool wind in our faces felt good as we walked up the hill. Moonlight turned everything around us into silver ghosts.

Alisha giggled. "What if they really do think it's a bear? We're being kind of mean you know, Nikki."

"No, we're not. We'll tell them it was us. Sh..sh.... We're getting close," I whispered, as we left the road to walk behind the Brown's garage. I could see the front of the tent.

As we were about to step out around the corner of the garage, I stopped short. I suppose you might call it a premonition, but something just didn't feel right. The hairs on the back of my neck bristled and stood to attention. Alisha's hand grabbed mine. I looked at her without speaking. She felt it too.

Hanging onto each other tightly, we craned our necks out around the corner of the garage. I stared into the semi-darkness of the yard for a few seconds, but I could find nothing wrong. As I made a move to step out, Alisha yanked my arm so hard I nearly fell over. Her other hand was over her mouth. She pointed into the yard, her finger bobbing up and down wildly.

From behind a pile of lumber near the tent, a black shadow lumbered. I blinked my eyes in disbelief and then froze in horror.

"It's a bear. Let's get out of here!" Alisha whispered frantically in my ear, as she tugged at my arm.

I pulled back. "Just a minute," I whispered. "It's headed toward the tent. We can't leave the boys!" I eyed the open stretch of yard between us and the house and wondered how far I could run towards it before the bear could catch up with me. I didn't know if there was a cub with it, but I knew if you ever got between a cub and its mother, you were in real trouble.

We watched in frozen silence as the bear meandered over to the tent with its nose against the ground. It nosed along the side of the tent, and then moved up to where I knew the boys' heads must be. I held my breath, my heart pounding against my rib cage.

I had to take the risk. Trevor wouldn't stand a chance of getting away if the bear should suddenly attack. I took a last gulp of fresh air and pulled my arm free of Alisha's grasp. I began running.

"GET LOST!" Trevor's voice suddenly thundered from inside the tent. Then there was a resounding SMACK, and by the time I'd raced into the middle of the yard and could see what was happening, the bear was galloping away towards the trees as fast as his legs would go.

Alisha had reached my side and we watched, stunned by the sudden turn of events. The bear was quickly swallowed up in the blackness of the forest.

There was a commotion inside the tent, and Trevor pulled himself out with Shawn close behind.

"Nikki, where are you? I hope I didn't hurt you, but I was mad..."

"Trevor, Shawn, are you guys okay?" we both chorused, as we arrived in front of the tent.

"The bear didn't hurt you, did he?" I asked. Just then, the lights went on in the house, and Shawn's dad stuck his head out of the door.

"Bear! Nice try, Nikki. We figured you might try something like that. The next time you pretend to be a bear, don't snort and snuffle so much. That's what really gave you away," Trevor said, with disgust.

"We decided to ignore you," Shawn put in. He looked a bit grumpy, as if he hadn't enjoyed the idea of someone playing a trick on him.

"But when you started poking at our faces, I'd had enough!" Trevor went on.

"What did you do?" I gasped.

Shawn's father had arrived moments before, clad in his pyjamas with a flashlight in his hand. I knew he would have something to say to us in a moment, but right now, he couldn't get a word in edgewise. He clicked his flashlight on and walked around the tent.

"I hit you with Shawn's book. I'm sorry. I didn't mean to hit you so hard."

Mr. Brown came around the edge of the tent, shining his flashlight at the ground. "Trevor, I think what you hit was a bear's nose, and from the look of these tracks, he was a big one too. A big, black bear, I'd say."

Trevor's eyes grew wide as he stared at the bear tracks. "You mean, there really was a bear," he said in a thin voice, "and I scared him away?"

"That's what we've been trying to tell you," Alisha said. "We came up to scare you, but when we got here, we saw the bear right at the head of your tent." She laughed. "You should have seen him run when you hit him. He took off like he'd been shot!"

I didn't dare look at Mr. Brown while Alisha

admitted why we had come up. Now we were probably in big trouble. But he didn't seem to hear her. He was still looking at the tracks.

"He sure was a big one all right. Look, I'm sure he won't come back tonight, but we're not going to take any chances. As soon as I drive the girls home, I'll help move your sleeping bags and things up onto the sundeck. It won't be quite like sleeping in a tent, but at least I know you'll be safe."

"So you came up to frighten the boys, eh?" Mr. Brown's voice suddenly boomed. Then he chuckled. "That reminds me of the time I was a Boy Scout and we raided the Girl Guide's camp which was down the creek from us."

"What happened?" we chorused.

"Well, when we arrived, there was no one at the camp. We were so surprised that we didn't do anything. We were halfway back to our camp before we realized what had probably happened. By the time we got to our camp, they'd pulled down all our tents and thrown our underwear in the creek."

"Didn't you retaliate?" Shawn asked, as we all laughed.

"No, we couldn't. They pulled up stakes and left the next morning."

"We don't need a ride home, Mr. Brown. Really we don't." I was pretty sure my dad had never raided any Girl Guide camp, and that he wouldn't be very understanding about what we'd just done.

Mr. Brown must have known what I was thinking. "Tell you what. I won't use the headlights. I don't need them anyway— and I won't drive into your yard. I'll just let you off at the gate. But I do insist on seeing you safely back. Even though it's not far, you two can't go traipsing around at this time of the night." He glanced at his watch. "My gosh, it's nearly one o'clock. Let's go."

"You guys were right, I guess...", Trevor said as we left, "about the food. We had a couple of cookies with us in the tent. He must have smelled them."

I looked at Alisha quickly. Neither one of us said anything, but we were probably thinking the same thing. If a little old cookie had brought the bear down from the woods, what would the scent of salt and vinegar chips do? He was probably up in the trees right now, standing on his hind legs, waving his nose in the air and trying to decide which direction those wonderful salt and vinegar smells were wafting from. He'd probably even risk another smack on the nose for that.

"Come on, let's hurry." I grabbed Alisha's arm, as we shouted our "good-byes" and headed for the car.

Mr. Brown let us off, as he had promised, at

the gate, and like ghosts we silently slipped back to the tent. I let Wagner out of the garage and muzzled his nose with my hand to keep him from barking. He wriggled instead.

"Phew! I'm not sleeping in here, that's for sure," Alisha muttered, as we eyed the inside of the tent. There were chips everywhere and the smell of them was very strong. I was pretty sure that old bear was on his way down here, right at this moment.

"Let's just sleep in my room," I suggested.

We tiptoed over to the basement door. It was locked! We usually locked the doors at night, but I hadn't thought they'd lock them when we were outside. I felt slightly offended. My mind's eye saw the bear getting closer. Another solution sprang to mind.

"Quick, let's get the aluminium ladder and climb up to the sundeck," I whispered to Alisha. Mom had had to get into the house that way once. It was kind of funny seeing her go over the railing in high heels. "We'll just drag our sleeping bags up and sleep up there."

We slipped back out to the garage and pulled the extension on the ladder, so we wouldn't make any noise at the house. Then, as quietly as we could, we carried it over to the house and propped it against the railing of the sundeck. There was a dull "clunk" as metal hit metal. I held my breath and waited for the lights to come on, but they didn't. So far, so good.

I went halfway up the ladder. As Alisha was handing me a sleeping bag, I thought I heard a car coming up our road. It seemed strange because there were no car lights. Once in a while, a car came up late at night, and when they found it was a dead end road, they turned around and left. I just hoped they wouldn't wake Mom and Dad.

I deposited the first sleeping bag onto the sundeck. Alisha gave me the second one, and I had one leg over the railing with her close behind, when Wagner let out a threatening growl.

Suddenly, there was a red light throbbing at us from the driveway, and we were blinded by a glaring spotlight.

"FREEZE! Don't move," boomed a voice through a megaphone from behind the light.

We froze!

An RCMP officer stepped in front of the light. "What are you kids doing?" he demanded. Then a bunch of lights came on, and the sliding door opened. Mom and Dad stumbled out.

"Nikki! Alisha! What on earth are you doing? There was a car at the driveway a short while ago with no headlights, and then we heard someone try the door. We were sure it was a burglar, and with you girls sleeping in the tent down there, we didn't want to take any chances."

The RCMP officer looked up at my dad. "I gather you know these girls, sir?" he asked, switching off the spotlight.

My dad ran his fingers through his hair. "Yes, yes, I know them. You'd better come up. I'm sure there's a very good story behind all this."

I tried to make sure that it sounded like the bear was to blame for everything. Dad had a rather amused look on his face when I mentioned that we had gone to "check" on the boys.

After I was all done talking, the RCMP officer stood up and put his hat back on. "Well, sir, I don't suppose you want to press charges," he said with a small smile.

Dad cleared his throat and scowled at us momentarily. "No, that won't be necessary. Thank you for coming out."

Dad agreed that the bear just might be tempted back by the salt and vinegar chip odour, so he helped us move everything, including the tent, back into the basement. We left it in a big heap to sort out in the morning. By the time we had finished, it was nearly 2:30 in the morning, and Alisha and I were struggling to keep awake.

Mom and Dad poked their heads in my door. "For the second time tonight, good night, girls. By the way," Dad said with a twinkle in his eye, "did I ever tell you about the time I was a Boy Scout, and we raided the Girl Guide's camp?" I looked at him in disbelief.

105

"Not now, dear," Mom said over his shoulder. "It's 2:30 in the morning. Besides, I don't think the girls are old enough for that story."

I smiled a sleepy smile and snuggled down into the blankets. "Good night, Mom. Good night, Dad...and thanks!"

Chapter 14

I thought that our night escapade might ruin our chance to go camping, but it didn't. We decided to go on the following Monday when there would be fewer tourists and it would be easier getting into the campground. Dad's only comment the day after the bear episode was that he was surprised the bear had actually come into the Brown's yard. I was quite happy to leave it at that.

Trevor just couldn't get over the fact that he'd been the one to scare the bear away. After three or four tellings, it sounded as if he'd known it was a bear all along, and that when he clouted it on the snout with Shawn's book, it was a real act of heroism.

I got tired of hearing about it. But I've got to admit, it seemed to cause a bit of a change in Trevor. He didn't seem to slouch in his chair as much, and there was a sparkle in his eyes that hadn't been there before. I wished he'd realize that there were other things he was capable of doing, like improving his reading. I talked about it with Shawn when we went riding a couple of days later.

"Sure, he could read better if he'd put his mind to it," Shawn said, as we trotted towards home. For our first ride, I'd taken Shawn on one of my favourite trails up along the power line. Ginger and Star, after some initial squealing and stamping of feet to determine that Ginger really was the boss, had settled into a comfortable companionship. Now they blew softly as they danced along the trail beside one another.

"You know how Mrs. Pearson had us buddy reading with the Grade threes at the end of the year. Why wouldn't that work with Trevor?" I said.

"Yeah, it probably would, but I don't think he'd want to read Beatrix Potter books the way they did." We both laughed.

I thought for a moment. "No, but I'll bet he'd enjoy *The Hobbit*," I said, thinking of the dragon in the story, and remembering Trevor's fascination with the dragon in the clouds that we'd seen.

"*The Hobbit*? Yeah, that's a great book. It's kind of long, though."

"Well, if we get him interested in a good story, he may want to read more things on his own," I thought aloud.

"I'll help too...if he'll let me," Shawn offered, as we arrived back in his yard.

The opportunity to introduce Trevor to *The Hobbit* came the next night while we were packing to go camping the next morning. I was making a pile of my stuff next to his near the door. Trevor had been ready for hours, and now he was wheeling back and forth talking to Mom as she bustled about. A couple of times, she had turned to do something and tripped over his chair. Finally, I heard her voice sounding a bit tired.

"No, I don't think there'll be bears in this campground, but we'll have to be very careful about making sure that there's no food in the tents." She walked around his chair again to go down the hall to the linen closet. "Uh, Trevor...why don't you go and see how Uncle Jim is doing. Maybe you could help him."

Trevor wheeled over to the door just as I was depositing some books on the top of my pile.

I held up *The Hobbit*. "Hey Trevor, here's a book I think you'd enjoy reading. I could help you."

Trevor snorted, as he flipped through it. "Ha, fat chance! Look at the size of it." He handed it back to me.

I tried again. "It's about a dragon. I know you'd like it. Besides, you already wrote to your mom that I was teaching you to read." I stopped in dismay. I hadn't meant to say that.

Trevor faced me angrily. "You snooped in my letter, didn't you? Well for your information, I didn't mean books. I was talking about the day we watched the clouds and how you showed me how to find shapes in them. I was telling her that you were teaching me to read clouds."

He abruptly turned and went out the door.

I'd done it again. I'd gone about things the wrong way. I plunked myself into the nearest chair and thought hard. I was pretty sure that Trevor was more annoyed than really mad at me, but I decided I did owe him an apology. I would do that later when he'd cooled off a bit. I was also pretty sure that I could win Trevor over to wanting to read the book I'd chosen, if I approached it the right way.

I got up and started packing again. I always think better when I'm busy with my hands. Before I went to bed that night, I had a new plan. I even talked it over with Dad. He thought it might work.

Chapter 15

It promised to be another hot, sunny Okanagan day as we squeezed into the car early the next morning.

"It's a good thing that Shawn decided to stay home and ride his horse. If he had come too, we'd have had to pull a trailer," Dad said, looking in his rear-view mirror at Alisha, Trevor, Wagner and me stuffed into the back seat along with a bunch of sleeping bags and pillows.

Wagner stood up and slurped Alisha on the ear while his tail wagged in my face. I gave him a push and he scrambled onto Trevor's knee and then hung his head out the window, panting happily. He loved car rides, and he probably sensed that this was something even more special.

"Did you remember Wagner's leash, Jim?"

Mom asked anxiously, as we pulled out of the driveway.

Dad rolled his eyes. "I remembered everything!"

We all settled down for a few seconds of companionable silence. I dug down beside me on the seat and retrieved my book. "Dad, can I read to you while you drive?" I asked.

Dad caught my eye in the rear-view mirror and smiled. "Sure Nikki. You know I always like to hear you read."

I flipped quickly to the first page. "In a hole in the ground there lived a hobbit," I began. I could feel Alisha's eyes on me, but I ignored her and kept on reading. On the other side of me, Trevor stared out of the window and stroked Wagner's head. I knew he was listening.

Hooray! The first part of my plan was working. I figured if I got Trevor in a spot where he couldn't get away, and he heard the beginning of the book, he'd be hooked.

As we pulled into the park, I shut the book. Trevor reached for the door handle. "What's the name of that book?" he asked.

"It's the one I told you about with a dragon in it. It's called *The Hobbit*. Do you like it?" I asked casually.

"Yeah, it's not bad. Maybe you could read some more of it later."

"Sure," I replied, grabbing Wagner by the collar as Alisha opened the door. I smiled at her as we climbed out, and she nodded. She was now in on the plan too.

Even though we were arriving early, we had to wait until someone left. Then we found a campsite on the third row up from the lake. Trevor helped set up the tent that he and Mom and Dad were going to sleep in, and Alisha and I set up ours a few feet away.

I crawled around the inside, sniffing carefully. I couldn't detect any residue of salt and vinegar smell, but if I did, I was going to sleep in the car. No one was going to have to persuade me not to have any food inside our tent tonight.

After we set up camp, we got into our bathing suits.

"Mom, will you watch Wagner if I tie him to a tree while we go down to the lake?" I asked. Wagner cocked his head and sat down awaiting his fate.

Mom backed out of the tent. "Yes, that will be fine. We'll be down a little later."

"Be careful on the road, kids," Dad said, as he settled into his lawn chair beside Wagner in the shade. "There are a couple of blind corners between here and the lake."

"We'll be careful!" Trevor caught my eye and we both grinned. It seemed like it didn't matter how old you were, parents were always giving reminders.

There was a lot of noise coming from around

the first corner, and when we rounded the bend, we saw why. In the first campsite was a tent trailer and a large camper van. Spilling in and out and all around were kids— I quickly counted six of them— ranging down from a boy a few years younger than us, to a little girl waddling around in diapers. A very tired-looking Mom was busy getting snacks onto the table for everyone.

"Wow," muttered Alisha, after we passed them, "I can't imagine having five brothers and sisters."

"Just think what it would be like babysitting them," I said, and for the rest of our walk we thought of different ways that six kids could probably drive a babysitter crazy.

By the time Mom and Dad walked down with Wagner to tell us it was lunch time, we'd all had enough sun and were tired of the water. After lunch, we decided to sit in the shade and play Rummy with the deck of cards I'd brought.

"Nikki, read some more of that book, will you?" Trevor asked quietly, after our third game of cards. "Sure," I said, "but I'm getting a sore throat. I won't be able to read for long."

Alisha headed for the tent and soon I saw her feet sticking out, kicking back and forth as she lay reading. She'd probably decided she'd heard me read out loud enough for one day.

I read to Trevor until a really exciting part was coming up. Suddenly, I stopped and put the book marker in. I clutched at my throat. "I can't read any more— my throat hurts too much," I said.

"You can't stop now," Trevor insisted.

I opened the book again. "Here, you read it. I'll just fill in the words you can't get." Trevor hesitated. Then he took the book from me and, a moment later, started reading.

"There was a most spe... spe...."

"Specially", I filled in.

"There was a most specially greedy, strong and w... w...."

"Wicked", I said.

"There was a most specially greedy, strong and wicked dragon called Sm... Sm...."

"Smaug. The dragon's name was Smaug," I carried on.

"Smaug," Trevor repeated, and then he slowly continued. "One day, he flew up into the air and came sou... th. The first we he... heard of it was a no... noise like a hur... hur... "

"Hurricane," I said.

"Hurricane coming from the No... North, and the pine-trees on the Mou... Mountain crea... creaking and cra... cracking in the w... wind."

Between the two of us, it sounded like pretty smooth reading. When we finished the page, I jumped back with my finger to a couple of the words I'd had to fill in for Trevor. He read them with a bit of help.

"Hey you're remembering these words pretty quickly, Trevor," I said.

Dad walked over and clapped him on the shoulder. "Sounds good, Trevor. All you need is a bit of practise."

Trevor beamed. "You think so? Actually, this isn't so bad." He turned the page and we started off again. By the time we had finished a chapter and decided to quit, I really was getting a sore throat, but I knew my plan was working. Tomorrow or the next day, as soon as he was willing to admit that we were actually working to improve his reading, I'd get him to start writing about the story as Dad had suggested. For a while though, I was going to play him like a fish on a long loose line.

Chapter 16

The excitement happened while I was having a sleep in the tent later that afternoon. Not only did I have a sore throat by the time I quit reading with Trevor, but my head had begun to ache, too. I decided to rest in the tent beside Alisha, who was still engrossed with her book. Wagner crawled in beside me and flopped down with his wet nose resting on my legs so he could catch the breeze from the doorway.

The smell of the hot tent, the muffled sounds of campers chopping wood and the persistent scolding of a robin nearby made me feel drowsy. Sprays of dappled sunlight tap danced silently across the tent's ceiling as breezes swept through the trees overhead. Soon, my eyes closed unwillingly and I slept.

* * *

"Nikki?" The wheel of Trevor's chair bumped

against my foot and jolted me awake. I shook my head groggily as I tried to figure out where I was.

"Nikki, come out. I want you to meet someone." Trevor's voice was persistent, and I could tell he was excited about something. I rubbed the sleep out of my eyes and looked around. Alisha was gone, and as I peered through the tent screening, it looked as if Mom and Dad and Wagner were gone too. I wondered how long I'd been sleeping. I tried to swallow. My throat felt as if it were on fire and my head as if a giant toad were sitting on it. I crawled out of the tent, squinting into the bright sunlight.

"Nikki, this is Mr. Stilmore, and this is Mandy. I just saved Mandy's life!" burbled Trevor, all in one breath.

"You what?" I asked, looking from Trevor's excited face to the man standing behind Trevor's chair, holding a toddler. It was the toddler in diapers that we'd seen earlier at the campsite around the bend.

The man extended his hand to me and pumped mine vigorously. The little girl he was holding chuckled and clapped her hands.

"Hi, Nikki," he said. "Please call me Jack. Your brother did save Mandy's life a few minutes ago, and I just wanted to tell your family how grateful we all are."

I didn't bother to correct him. I suddenly felt weak in the knees. I sank onto the bench of the picnic table that was nearby.

"But how?" I gasped. "What happened?"

Trevor looked up at Jack and then over at me. "Well, Alisha went back down to the beach, and then Auntie Kay and Uncle Jim took Wagner for a walk. I was playing Solitaire and when I finished, you were still asleep, so I decided to go back down to the beach. As I went around that sharp bend in the road, I saw Mandy wandering in the middle of the roadway. I could hear a car coming down behind me quite fast..."

"So he crossed over the road and scooped Mandy out of the way, even though he was putting himself in danger of being run over," Jack interrupted. "It was a very heroic thing to do." He clapped Trevor on the shoulder. "You sure can move in that chair, son. I've never seen anything like it!"

Jack looked at me. "I have a brother who is physically challenged as well. He lives here in Kelowna." Suddenly his face lit up. He looked at Trevor again. "Say, that gives me an idea..."

Just then, Mom and Dad and Alisha arrived back. As I went over to tell them the exciting news, I heard Trevor explain to Jack that he was a cousin of mine rather than a brother and that he was just visiting us from the Prairies. I felt a bit disappointed. I was so proud of Trevor at that moment, that I would have been happy to have had him for a brother.

Mom and Dad and Alisha were introduced to Jack, and Trevor retold the story to them.

"I'm amazed at how fast this boy moves in his chair and how well he manoeuvres it," Jack said to Mom and Dad, when Trevor was finished. "I was just telling the kids about my brother who lives in Kelowna," he went on. "He works for 'People in Motion'."

Trevor frowned. "What's 'People in Motion'?" he asked.

"It's an organization that promotes sports activities for the physically challenged. The B.C. Games for the Physically Disabled are held once a year somewhere in B.C. This year, they're here in Kelowna. My brother, Cyril, is a coach. I know one of his athletes can't make it, and he might be able to put you in his place... if he times you and you qualify," Jack said.

"Me?" Trevor's eyes opened wide. "What's it all about?"

"Well, there are several events. There are team sports like basketball..."

"Trevor's pretty good at basketball," I said.

"I'll bet he is," Jack replied. "Unfortunately, those teams have been practising together for some time now. But the athlete who can't make it was in track. You'd probably do well in that."

Trevor's face began to turn crimson. "Me?" he croaked again. "Oh, no...uh, I wouldn't be any good at that." He wheeled around so that nobody could see his face. I could almost hear his heart thumping. I know mine was.

Jack cleared his throat. Mandy squirmed in his arms, demanding to be put down. He glanced at Mom and Dad and then at me. "Well, it's something for you to think about. It's kind of fun, even if you don't win."

He shifted Mandy onto his other arm and rummaged in his shirt pocket for a notepad and pen. He put his foot up on the seat of the picnic table I was sitting on and scribbled something onto the paper on his knee. He laid it on the table beside Trevor and put a small rock on it to hold it down. "There's my brother's number, if you should change your mind." He rested his hand lightly on Trevor's shoulder for a moment. "I really can't express it in words, but thank you again."

He said goodbye to Mom and Dad and was about to leave. Suddenly, a gust of wind swept through the campsite. The paper on the table rattled and lifted. The pebble began to dance off the paper. Trevor's hand shot out and clamped down on it. He didn't pick it up, but he slid the book we'd been reading on top of it, so that it wouldn't blow away. He turned slightly. "Thanks, Mr. Stilmore," he said quietly.

"No problem," Jack said. He lifted Mandy high in the air and whistled a tune to her as he walked down the road to his own campsite.

Everyone was silent for a few moments. Then I saw Mom looking at me.

"Nikki, do you feel all right? You look terrible."

I did not feel all right. In fact, I felt terrible! But I wasn't about to spoil the camping trip I'd been wanting to go on.

"I'm okay. Maybe I had a bit too much sun this morning," I said.

She walked over to me and placed a cool hand on my forehead. It felt wonderful. "You feel awfully hot. I think you have a fever." She looked at Dad, who made a face.

"Oh no, we forgot the thermometer. I was sure we must have brought everything in the house but the kitchen sink."

"Very funny," Mom scolded. She looked at me again. "I'll get you a wet cloth for your head, and we'll see how you are this evening."

After supper, I was no better. The light from the camp fire hurt my eyes so much that I sat with my sunglasses on, huddled inside a blanket, while the rest of the family roasted marshmallows and popped corn. Finally, I excused myself and went to bed.

My night was filled with wild images that made me toss and turn. Huge, hairy bears, with mouths full of gleaming teeth and salt and vinegar potato chips, were all mixed up with cars screeching around corners, bearing down on Trevor who was sitting in the middle of the road, white-faced and terrified.

"Nikki, stop moaning in my ear. You must be having a nightmare," Alisha whispered, as she shook me in the middle of the night. "Wow, you're boiling! Are you all right? Should I get your mom?" she asked in a worried voice.

"No," I muttered, "don't get Mom. I'll be all right by morning."

But in the morning, I still had the headache, sore throat and fever. When Mom looked inside the tent she gasped. "Oh, Nikki! You're covered with spots. No wonder you've been feeling so rough. You must have the chickenpox. We'd better get you home, pronto."

"Chickenpox!" Alisha wrinkled her nose. "Gross!"

Mom smiled at her. "Don't say too much about them, Alisha dear. You'll probably catch them, too."

She looked at me again. "I wonder if Trevor's had chickenpox," she mused.

"Why?" I asked. "What difference does it make?"

"If Trevor catches chickenpox, he won't be able to go in the B. C. Games, even if he decides he wants to," she said thoughtfully.

Chapter 17

Mom was right. By the next week, Alisha was down with chickenpox, too. By that time, I was over the worst of it. I felt better, but I still had lots of spots and Mom wouldn't let me go out anywhere.

We hadn't been able to find out about Trevor though. He couldn't remember ever having had them. Mom had tried to phone Auntie Mary a few times to ask her, but there had been no answer.

"She must have gone away for a few days," Mom told Trevor. "We'll just have to watch for those red spots to appear."

During the week I'd been in bed, Trevor had spent a lot of time reading *The Hobbit* with me. The more we read the story, the more I could see that Trevor was a lot like the Hobbit. Neither the Hobbit nor Trevor had ever had many exciting things happen to him. When the pack of dwarves came along and coaxed the Hobbit to go on adventures, I thought of Shawn and Alisha and myself. I could certainly see myself as Gandalf, the wizard who performed magic and whose power was stronger than anyone else's. It wasn't likely, though, that Trevor would become a hero in the end the way the Hobbit had.

I also had him writing about different things in the story. Some of his descriptions were becoming pretty good. Dad had offered to set aside some time each night, if Trevor wanted to, to help him in reading, writing and math. Much to our surprise, he had agreed. He hadn't mentioned the B. C. Games again, though.

When he wasn't spending time with me that week, he was up at Shawn's. I wondered what they were spending their time doing, because I knew Shawn would be eager to spend as much time with his new horse as possible.

One afternoon, Trevor came in to see me when he got home from Shawn's. He tossed a book down beside me on the bed. "That's what I'm starting to read by myself. It's a Hardy Boy mystery. I borrowed it from Shawn."

I tried not to look as if I'd just won a contest. "Good for you," I said, and then I yawned. There was something in Trevor's face that told me he was happy with himself for more than choosing a new reading book.

"What have you two been up to every day,

anyway?" I asked suspiciously.

Trevor looked at me a moment as if he were wondering how much he could trust me.

"Nikki, can you keep a secret?" he whispered, as he wheeled up close to my bed.

I snorted. "Of course I can! What's so special that it has to be kept secret?"

A grin lit up Trevor's face, and his eyes sparkled. He leaned forward. "I've been riding Shawn's horse."

I sat bolt upright. "You've been riding Shawn's horse? How can you?"

Trevor glanced over his shoulder. "Sh...sh...I don't want Auntie Kay to hear. She'd probably be afraid I'd get hurt."

I lowered my voice. "But how do you do it?" I whispered.

"I decided it wasn't fair that you and Shawn were having all the fun. Shawn was always riding when I went up there, so one day, when his parents weren't home, I convinced him to double me. It took us quite a while to get me on the first time, but now we've got a system worked out, and I can get on a lot quicker."

I threw back the covers and sat on the edge of the bed. "You mean you've been doing this all week?"

Trevor laughed. "Yeah. In fact, today we even galloped. My balance is pretty good, and I had Shawn to hang on to." His face clouded over.

"Oh yeah, that reminds me. I think Shawn is getting the chickenpox. When we got back today, he had a headache and sore throat, the same as you did last week."

"Trevor," Mom's voice called. "There's a phone call for you. I think it's that Mr. Stilmore." She waited for Trevor to get past her and then came into the room. "Nikki, you look like you're feeling better."

I stood up and grabbed the hair brush and ran it through my hair. "Yeah, I am suddenly feeling quite a bit better." I paused, my hairbrush in midair. "Mr. Stilmore's on the phone, eh? I bet I know why. I wonder what Trevor will say?"

We soon found out. Trevor appeared at the doorway. "Auntie Kay, if I get to go in the B.C. Games, will you or Uncle Jim be able to drive me in to practises?"

With Mom's assurance that it would be possible, he disappeared again. A few minutes later, he was back.

"Trevor," I squealed, "what made you decide to do it after all?"

Trevor laughed and did a wheelie in the middle of my room. "Well, part of me wanted to right from the start— I just didn't think that I could win. Then I started to realize it didn't really matter if I won or not, that it would probably be a fun thing to do, just as Mr. Stilmore said. But by that time, I was worried I might come down with the chickenpox, and I didn't want to get everyone's hopes up and then disappoint them."

"The Games are in a few weeks, aren't they? It doesn't leave much time to practise, does it?" Mom asked thoughtfully.

Trevor grinned again. "Well, I've sort of been practising on my own. I time myself and see how fast I can get up to Shawn's place each day. I figure no course is going to be harder than that hill. I also told Shawn what I was thinking of doing, and we set up a bit of a course in his yard, just for fun." He laughed. "I do it in my chair and Shawn does it on his horse."

I sniffed. "You rat. All these secrets you've been keeping from me." I enjoyed watching Trevor squirm for a moment as he worried about my telling Mom that he'd been riding Shawn's horse. But of course, I wasn't about to tell. I was anxious to see him ride for myself. I winked at him, to let him know I was just kidding.

"Okay, clear out everybody. I want to get dressed. I'm tired of being sick," I said, as I shooed them out and shut the door.

Although I wasn't allowed to go, over the next few days either Dad or Mom would take Trevor to town to practise on the track at the Apple Bowl. He had more than met the qualification time and had been slated to go in the 800 and the 400 metre track events. He learned that there would be four or five other kids he'd be racing against.

"Most of them I can beat hands down," Trevor told me one evening.

"How do you know?" I asked.

"Some of them are from around here and I've been watching them practise. Besides, Mr. Stilmore's brother, Cyril, knows most of them and he says my time is much better." He frowned. "There's one kid though from Prince George who will be here. His name is Scott Smith— he's pretty fast, and he's older than me."

Trevor was really impressed with Mr. Stilmore's brother, Cyril, who was lending him the special track chair he was going to be racing in, as well as coaching him.

"You should see him, Nikki," Trevor said. "He's big and blonde and good looking, and he has muscles out to here. He was injured in a skiing accident ten years ago. When you do really well at the provincial level, you can go on to the Canadian Nationals. He's even won gold medals there!"

"Wow!" I breathed. I was glad to be getting all this information. I was getting awfully bored staying home. I couldn't even go to Shawn's or Alisha's since they were now sick, too.

On the Wednesday night before the weekend

B. C. Games, we finally got hold of Trevor's mom on the phone. She talked to Mom first, and we learned that Trevor had had chickenpox when he was in kindergarten, so we didn't have to worry any more about that.

Then Trevor got to talk to her. He told her all about the sleepover at Shawn's and clouting the bear on the nose, then about our camping trip and saving Mandy, and how he was practising to go in 'some games' this week-end.

I tried not to eavesdrop, but I noticed he tried to downplay the importance of the Games, and I also noticed that he never mentioned the tutoring help he was getting. Maybe there were too many things happening to Trevor all at once. Perhaps he wasn't sure that he'd be successful at all of them.

When he got off the phone, he was excited.

"Guess what? Mom may be coming out in a few weeks. She's been spending some time with Dad. She told me he said to say 'Hi' and that he misses me." He wheeled around so that his face was away from me. "If they get back together again, I guess they'll both be out...and I'll be going back with them."

He wheeled over towards the door without looking at any of us. "If my dad misses me so much, I wonder why he didn't phone and say so." I started to follow him, but the look on Mom's face told me not to.

When he was out of earshot, she said, "Trevor just needs to be alone for awhile. I'm not so sure he even knows what he wants to happen with his mom and dad at this point."

Chapter 18

"No, for the last time, I'm not going to let you ride Ginger the night before your big race. You might hurt yourself, and then it would be my fault." Trevor just smiled at me as he leaned forward to watch me finish cinching up the saddle, his arms on the bottom rail of the fence. Wagner sat beside him, panting happily.

This had all started half an hour ago, when Mom and Dad had left to go grocery shopping, and I had decided to go for a ride.

My spots had finally disappeared. I'd even been allowed to go in and watch Trevor practise at the Apple Bowl and meet Jack Stilmore's brother.

"You're right about Cyril Stilmore. He's quite a hunk!" I admitted.

"Stop trying to change the subject, Nikki. Come on, I've done it a thousand times with Shawn. I won't fall off. I promise."

I snorted. "How many times have you ridden with Shawn?" I asked knowingly.

"Well, at least six or seven. Look, it's easy. Just take her over there where her back is lower than the fence. I'll pull myself up onto the fence, and then you push me over and on to the saddle. It'll work, I tell you."

I could tell there was no use arguing with him any more. He had done it before, and besides, I did want to see how he did it.

"Okay, okay," I muttered. "Get over here." I led Ginger over to a low spot. Trevor wheeled over to the other side of the fence and hoisted himself up, grunting and turning red in the face with the exertion. Finally, he had his body level with the top rail. I held him steady and helped push him over. He was heavy, and I was almost unable to support his weight, but finally he was across. Then he grasped the saddle and pulled himself up. With his hands, he placed one leg and then the other on either side of the horse. Ginger must have known something special was going on. She stood perfectly still, tight in along the fence.

"Whew! I forgot you're not as strong as Shawn. I didn't think I was going to make it for a moment," Trevor gasped. He wiped his arm across his forehead that was damp with perspiration.

"Yeah, well, you're on now. I hope you're okay,"

I muttered. I knew this had been a foolish idea, and I was glad he was safely on. I climbed on in front of him. I was surprised. His balance was quite good, even though his legs couldn't grip. He was hanging onto me to help himself, but he wasn't clutching at me.

This was kind of fun. I'd have to ask Dad to think of an easier way to get Trevor on and off. Off! Oh my gosh, I hadn't thought of how we'd get him off.

Ginger walked along the overgrown trail that runs behind our place. Ripe, purple Saskatoons hung in bunches along the side of the trail, begging to be picked. Trevor grabbed at a bunch and snapped them off as we went by. I could hear him slurping them in my ear, and a moment later, he dangled some in front of my nose.

"They're good! Want some?" he asked. I saw a tiny spider on one of the berries and part of a sticky white web stuck to another. The thought of the whole mess in my braces didn't help.

"Uh, no thanks," I replied.

I reached out and flicked a mosquito from Ginger's right ear. "So, now that you've watched this guy from Prince George, do you think you can beat him?" Scott Smith had been at the track this morning when we'd gone in to practise. He'd looked pretty fast to me.

Trevor stopped slurping his berries for a moment. "I don't know. Our times are similar, for the 800, but he does better than me on the 400. I guess I'm better at long distances." He laughed in my ear. "It must be from pushing myself up to Shawn's house."

The woody scent of pine was strong in the air. Ginger pricked up her ears as a squirrel raced up a nearby tree and perched on a limb above us, chattering madly as we passed underneath. Wagner scouted ahead of us, bushy tail disappearing and reappearing as he checked every opportunity to follow a new scent in the tall, weedy grass on either side of the trail.

"I wish we had places like this on the Prairies," Trevor said in my ear.

"You mean, you don't?" I said, somewhat surprised. I'd never been to the Prairies.

"Naw, just wide open fields with foxtail grass waving from the ditches. No squirrels either. Just funny, little gophers that pop their heads out of their holes and watch you with beady, black eyes. Then they flick their tail and they're gone."

Ginger grabbed a mouthful of tall broom grass that was growing on the trail. I flicked her with the reins. She knew she wasn't allowed to do that when she was being ridden.

I was curious. "Do you miss home?"

Trevor was silent for a moment. "Naw, not really. I don't miss the fights over me, that's for sure. I guess..."

I never found out what Trevor was about to say, for at that moment Wagner discovered a grouse hiding in the tall grass beside the trail. Without warning, she flew up in front of Ginger, wings beating the air loudly, her voice screeching in indignation.

Snorting with fear, Ginger jumped sideways and then reared. Before I could even think of what to do to save the situation, Trevor slid off Ginger's rear end, pulling me with him. He landed underneath me with a loud "Oomph."

I scrambled to my feet and squatted beside Trevor. He lay very still with his eyes closed. His face was colourless.

"Oh, please God, don't let him be hurt," I prayed, as I picked up his hand and rubbed it. "Trevor, are you okay?"

Ginger nuzzled my shoulder from behind. She seemed sorry for having caused us to fall off. Wagner bounded back towards us through the tall grass and stopped beside Trevor. With a whine, he started to lick Trevor's face.

"Yuk, Wagner, get lost," Trevor moaned, as he opened one eye and then the other.

I pushed Wagner away. "Are you okay? You're awfully white."

"I think so. I just got the breath knocked out of me." He pushed himself into a sitting position with his arms and winced. "My arm hurts a little."

I looked behind him at the rock which his arm must have hit when he landed. "Do you think it's broken?"

He moved it around and winced again. "No, it's not broken. I can move it." He looked at my face and must have realized how scared I was. "I'll be okay. Just a bit stiff for a few days probably."

I bit my lip as I thought of the race tomorrow. If Trevor's chances of going in it were ruined because I'd let him ride, I'd never forgive myself. "I'll go get your chair," I said, turning abruptly so that he wouldn't see how upset I was. I tied Ginger to a nearby tree and told Wagner to stay with Trevor. Then I raced back along the path to where we'd left the chair and quickly returned with it.

I noticed on the way back to the house that Trevor was favouring his arm a lot. Mom and Dad hadn't returned yet, thank heavens. I dumped some ice cubes into a plastic bag, wrapped them in a towel and brought them back out to Trevor for his arm to rest on.

I studied the maple leaves dancing in the breeze over Trevor's head. "What...what about the race tomorrow?" I asked.

"I'm going in that race no matter what happens," he said quietly.

We said no more about it. I certainly wasn't going to try and change his mind, not when I'd been working so hard to get him to gain confidence in himself. But I wondered what sort of shape he'd be in the next day.

When Mom and Dad arrived back with the groceries, Trevor disappeared into the basement. He wasn't around much after dinner either, and he said his "Good nights" early.

"He just wants to be well rested for tomorrow," I said to Mom and Dad, when I saw the surprised look on their faces. I hoped with all my heart that was true. A little while later, I slipped into his room with another ice pack, but he was already asleep.

Chapter 19

I awoke to the ominous sound of dripping eaves. Rain! I leapt out of bed and flung open the curtains of my window. Mountains of soft, white clouds hung suspended over the lake. Here and there, shafts of sunlight shot through the clouds, hanging golden curtains to the water. The air smelled crisp and damp, but it appeared as if the shower were over. By the time Trevor's race started, it surely would clear.

I didn't get a chance to talk to Trevor before we left, but I watched as he gobbled his breakfast down, to see if I could tell how his arm was feeling. I was pretty sure it was still bothering him.

When we arrived at the Apple Bowl at 8:30, already the air seemed filled with excitement. Colourful flags snapped in the breeze, and a huge banner saying "B.C. Games for the Physically Disabled" billowed over the entrance gate. Media people were setting up their cameras, and people with bright blue ribbons pinned to their chest scurried about organizing last minute details. We left Trevor with Cyril and headed up into the stands, as they were already beginning to fill up.

The clink of pop bottles and the mouthwatering odour of hamburgers and onions frying on an open grill reached me. I peered over the edge of the grandstand at the concession below.

I turned around and caught Mom's eye. "Can you lend me some money, please, and take it out of my allowance?"

"Oh Nikki, for goodness sake, sit down. It's only 9 o'clock. You just ate breakfast. You can't be hungry."

"I am hungry. I think I'm nervous. I always get hungry when I'm nervous," I replied.

I saw Dad sniff the air. "Those do smell awfully good. I must be nervous too." He smiled at Mom and reached into his pocket. "Do you want one too, Kay?" he asked, as he handed me a twenty dollar bill.

Mom rolled her eyes. Then she grinned and nodded. "We may as well all be crazy, I guess."

I was halfway down to the concession when they announced the National Anthem was to be sung, so I stopped and stood like everyone else. I always feel kind of special when I sing "O Canada", sort of the way I do when I've accomplished something big. Today I sang my heart out. I was fine until the second verse. When we started singing "God keep our land, Glorious and free", I suddenly looked down and caught sight of Trevor in his red nylon biking shirt that Mom had bought him. He was sitting tall and straight, facing the flag and singing. My throat got all tight feeling, and I couldn't sing any more. I looked away quickly. I wasn't about to cry in public!

When the anthem had finished, I ran down the rest of the stairs. I saw Alisha and Shawn and their families coming through the entrance gates. By shouting and waving, I caught their attention, and they made their way over to me.

"Hi, Nikki," Shawn said, smiling at me. I hadn't seen him since his bout with the chickenpox. He still had spots all over him, but I guess he was past the contagious stage. He actually seemed glad to see me.

The man in the concession booth handed me the hamburgers. Alisha gasped. "Nikki! Hamburgers? I've just had breakfast."

I laughed. "Me too, but we're all nervous. Maybe this will help."

The first race was being announced. "Come on, I'm sure there's room for you two up with us— if your parents don't mind finding their own spot." We started working our way back up the aisle.

"I'm nervous for Trevor too," Shawn said. "I hope he does okay in the 400."

I took a slurp of my cola. "I hope he does all right in both of them."

"But he can't, he's been deleted from the 800," Alisha's voice said from behind me.

"What!" I stopped so quickly that Alisha bumped into me. I whirled around, almost dropping the food tray.

"Didn't you know? Look at the information board. We saw it when we came in," Alisha said in a thin voice.

I glanced across the field to the information board, where the changes for each particular event were listed. Near the bottom it said: 800 metre— deleted— Trevor Manning.

"Oh no," I moaned. I slid onto a nearby bench for a moment to recuperate. I could pick Trevor out below in his red shirt and helmet, with number 23 on his front. Cyril was leading him through some warm-up activities. They had the athletes cordoned off from the public, and I knew I wouldn't be able to get to him.

"What could have happened?" Shawn muttered. "He was doing so well in his practises."

I was pretty sure that I knew what had happened. It had something to do with his arm, and with that crazy horseback ride I'd let him talk me into. I'd let it happen. Miss Know It All! Miss Gandalf the Magic Dwarf with power greater than anyone else's. How stupid could I be!

I stumbled up to where Mom and Dad were. I could tell by their faces that they'd seen the information board too and were as confused as Alisha and Shawn were. The smell of hamburgers suddenly made me sick. I handed the box of food to Dad and sat down, silent.

"Did you see the board, Nikki? What could have happened?" Dad craned his neck, trying to catch sight of Trevor. "I'd like to get down there and talk to him."

Mom placed a hand on Dad's arm. "There's no use us getting all in a tizzy. There must be a good reason for it. He's still in the 400. He'll do fine."

I sank lower onto the bench. He wouldn't do fine. Cyril must have noticed Trevor's arm and had probably told him he was deleting him in both races. Trevor, in his stubbornness—why, yesterday he'd said he was going in that race no matter what—had probably finally agreed to give up the longer one, realizing that he'd never be able to do both. But the 400 was his weakest, and now, with his injured arm, I just knew he didn't stand a chance.

The announcer had called for the 400. I looked down. They were taking their spots for a staggered start to go around the oval once. The one good thing I noticed was that Trevor had obtained the inside lane. Cyril had explained to us that it gives what is known as a psychological advantage. Everyone in the race goes the same distance, but it appears as if the distance is shorter on the inside lane. There were five athletes in the race. Two lanes over was Scott Smith.

I jumped as the starting gun suddenly went off. I closed my eyes and buried them behind my fists. The seconds ticked by, each one seeming to take an eternity. Mom and Dad and Alisha and Shawn were yelling their loudest. Then I felt them jump to their feet.

"Nikki!" Mom grabbed my arm. "Look! Trevor and that other boy are both pulling away from the rest."

I opened one eye. It was true. Number 23 in the red, which was Trevor, and number 49 in blue, who I knew was Scott Smith, were leaving the other three behind. They were directly opposite where they had started, so they were half way through the course. I looked at the scoreboard where the seconds were flashing by...59...60...1:01...1:02...1:03.

I leapt to my feet and shoved past Mom and Dad.

"Nikki, where are you going?" Dad called

after me. But I was already flying down the steps two at a time.

"Go, Trevor, go!" I screamed. I reached the barrier which separates the track from the spectators, pushed myself past some people and hung over the metal railing.

On the way down, I had seen Trevor take a slight lead. Now, as they came around the corner into the homestretch, he began to lag. His face was a mask of pain, his mouth held in a white, thin line. It was taking all of his strength just to keep going.

Scott Smith pulled out, a determined look on his face.

1:34...1:35...1:36 flashed the clock.

I leaned further over the railing and screamed once more, "Go, Trevor, go!" I saw him glance over at me, and for a second, our eyes locked.

"You can do it!" I shrieked in a high, wavery voice that threatened to give way to tears.

Suddenly, the image of the magnificent dragon we'd seen in the clouds that day, floated into my subconscious. A dragon sitting with folded wings, belching clouds of fire. Then, in my mind, I saw its wings unfold for flight. It became an elongated dragon, with wings and neck outstretched, soaring through a sapphire kingdom. Trevor had so much wanted to be like that dragon. And now I knew he could be!

"Go, Dragon, go!" I shouted. My voice became loud and strong. "GO, DRAGON, GO!"

The look on Trevor's face changed from pain to fierce determination. He gritted his teeth. His face was dripping with sweat, and his red shirt clung to his body, showing each bulging muscle as he pushed...pushed...pushed, and drew even once again with Scott.

1:44...1:45...1:46...1:47...and they were over the finish line.

I gripped the railing as the blood rushed to my head. It had been so close that I wasn't even sure who had won. I held my breath as the placement judges ran out on to the track.

A woman stepped in front of me, blocking my view. I pushed back in beside her. A hum filled the air as the microphone was turned on for an announcement. "Ladies and Gentlemen, we have just had a very close race here in our 400 metre event. In first place, by two-tenths of a second, we have Trevor Manning. Trevor Manning gets gold."

I grabbed the woman's arm, pumping it, as I jumped up and down shouting, "He did it! He did it!"

She looked down at me. "Yes, he certainly did!"

I brushed away the tears that were running down my face, and a loud sob escaped from my throat as I watched the judge place the gold medal around Trevor's neck. I tried to swallow over the lump that was sitting in the back of my throat. I looked up at the woman who was watching me curiously.

"That's my cousin who just won the gold medal in the 400 metre, at the B. C. Games!" I said proudly.

Then they were all behind me: Mom, Dad, Alisha and Shawn, and we were all hugging and shouting to Trevor, and giving him the thumbs up sign.

The media had Trevor and Scott over at the side now, taking pictures and interviewing both of them. I think Scott was really surprised when Trevor pushed past him at the last second, but he didn't appear to be too upset. He was smiling for the camera and the reporter, and a few seconds later, I saw him talking to Trevor.

We were about to make our way over to Trevor to congratulate him, when we saw Cyril motion to him. They both turned and headed over to the ambulance which was parked at the side near the entrance.

Just then, the announcer asked that people please return to their seats so that the next race could get underway.

It was with a great deal of alarm that Mom and Dad watched Trevor being loaded into the ambulance. Cyril turned and searched for us in the crowd. When he caught my dad's eye, he shouted, "We're going to the hospital. See you there."

It took me the whole trip to the hospital to explain to Mom and Dad what had happened the night before. They were not impressed!

Chapter 20

Mom and I jumped to our feet as Trevor appeared from the cubicle in Emergency, being pushed by a Doctor. He had a cast on his right arm and a sling going up and around his neck. Dad and Cyril quickly went over to shake hands with the Doctor and to talk to him.

Trevor took one look at our faces. "I'm okay, really I am! And it's not broken, Nikki," he said, as he saw my mouth open to protest.

"It's just a hairline fracture, but because I put so much pressure on it during the race, and because I have to use my arm all the time to push myself around, the doctor wanted to make sure that it heals properly."

The doctor looked down at Trevor and smiled. "Yes, I do want to make sure it heals properly, and that means that you're going to have to get used to being pushed for the next couple of days." He winked at Trevor. "And, no more horseback riding until that cast is off in a couple of weeks."

I glanced at Mom. She'd had a fit on the way to the hospital, just as I knew she would, when I'd told her what we'd been doing the night before.

"When you get the cast off," the doctor continued, "I think it's an excellent idea."

"You do?" Mom asked in disbelief.

The doctor smiled. "Sure! The more activities these youngsters can get involved in, the better. Trevor obviously had to have a lot of courage to try it. Anyone could have fallen off in the same manner and injured themselves."

The doctor bent over and tugged at the red and white ribbon until it came out from behind Trevor's sling. The glittering gold medal flopped out.

"Congratulations, Trevor. Most kids would have never had the guts to finish that race, never mind win a gold medal! I suspect I'll be reading about you in the newspaper tonight." He grabbed Trevor's left hand and shook it, lifting it in a high sign. Then he tousled his hair. "I'll see you in two weeks."

"Well, I think this calls for lunch out to celebrate," Dad said, stepping behind Trevor's wheelchair. "Can you join us, Cyril?"

Cyril smiled, "Sure, why not? It's not every day that one of my athletes wins gold." He glanced at his watch. "We'll still have time to get back and see the 800 this afternoon. I'd like to see how Scott's time is."

It was amazing how quickly my appetite returned. By the time my Teriyaki chicken burger with guacamole— that green squishy stuff that tastes so good— came, I was ravenous. Trevor was too. For a few minutes, we ate without speaking.

I stopped to lick some guacamole off my fingers. "You know, Trevor, you turned out to be like the Hobbit after all."

Trevor wrinkled his nose at me and snorted. "Oh yeah? Well, don't try calling me "Hobbit" or I'll have to call you "Jaws" again." We both laughed.

Dad cleared his throat. "Speaking of adventures and things like that, Trevor...can you be packed to go to the Prairies with me tomorrow?"

Trevor carefully laid his hamburger down. His eyes remained on his plate, and his shoulders slumped.

I jumped to my feet. "What! He doesn't have to go back already, does he?" I shouted. People at nearby tables looked over at us in alarm.

"Nikki, sit down, for Heaven's sake," Dad ordered. He looked at Trevor, who was still sitting staring at his plate. "Before you two turn into the 'Doom Gloom Twins', let me finish...please." He lowered his voice. "Trevor, your mom phoned last night after you were in bed. We had a long talk and she's...she's going to move out here for a fresh start. You'll both be staying with us for a while until we find her a house to rent. She needs you to come back and help her sort and pack things."

The freckles stood out on Trevor's face as he looked up. "She's moving here?" he said. There was a moment of silence. "What about my dad?"

Dad cleared his throat. "Well, son, it looks like your mom and dad aren't going to be together anymore."

Silence grew heavy at the table. I held my breath and watched Trevor as different emotions fluttered over his face. I still didn't know how he really felt about his mom and dad breaking up. Finally, Trevor looked around the table at us all. His eyes locked with mine.

"That's okay," he said slowly. "I used to think it was my fault they broke up...because of the accident...but now I think...well, I think they just don't belong together anymore."

My breath hissed out in relief. A small smile played at the corner of Trevor's mouth. Then his eyes lit up. "You mean, I'll be living out here for good?"

"Wow," I squealed. "That means you'll be going to our school."

The smile faded from Trevor's face. It was

going to be humiliating to be a grade behind us.

Dad put his hand up before anyone could open their mouth. "Hold it, hold it. I have some more good news. I've spoken to the principal, Trevor. She says if you continue to receive extra help, and if you work hard in school, she's willing to place you in grade seven in September."

Trevor's face split into a grin. "Really, you mean it? Oh wow!"

Cyril stood up. "Trevor, this is great news. It means you and I can continue to work together." He put his hand on Trevor's shoulder and looked him in the eye. "You know, Trevor, you have great potential. You seem to be a born athlete to have done so well this quickly. If you continue to work hard and have the proper coaching, the sky's the limit." He smiled. "You've got the Western Canada Games, the Canada Games, The Nationals, even some day the Olympics to shoot for. I wouldn't be a bit surprised if you made it that far."

Trevor's face really lit up. He seemed to glow. But he was at a loss for words and all he could say again was "Really, you mean it? Oh WOW!"

Cyril grinned. "Yes, I do mean it. As I said though, it will mean a tremendous amount of hard work and determination, and a lot of focusing on what you're trying to do. But if anybody can do it, I think you can!" He glanced at his watch. "You know folks, I hate to break up a good party, but if we're going to see that 800, we'd better hustle."

I looked down at our plates. Nobody had finished their meal because nobody had eaten since Dad started talking. I'd never seen such a day for losing appetites. I'd never seen such a day!

Chapter 21

I dropped the lipstick into my overnight bag and zipped it shut. My very own lipstick! Mom had bought it for me yesterday. It was a little present for helping her spend two days cleaning the basement for Trevor and his mom. I swore it was so clean and tidy that the Queen of England could comfortably move in.

Trevor and Dad had been gone for three days now. They were expected back the day after tomorrow.

I was getting ready to leave for Vancouver with Alisha and her parents to visit some friends of theirs for a couple of days. It had been awfully boring after Trevor left, even though Mom had kept me pretty busy, and I had gone riding with Shawn twice.

I don't know about Shawn, though. All he wants to do is ride horses, and all he wants to talk about is horses. He should know that when you're going into grade seven, there are other things in life besides horses.

I grabbed my bag and headed for the living room. I stopped to look in the mirror to make sure that none of my breakfast was stuck in my braces. Nothing is worse than talking to people who have that problem. I checked out the colour of the lipstick Mom had bought me. Not bad— even with braces.

The shrill of the telephone cut through the quiet house. I let it ring three times, waiting for Mom to answer it, but she didn't. She must have been in the garden.

I lifted the receiver on the fourth ring. "Hello? Oh hi, Cyril. No, they're not back yet. What?... Really!... You're kidding.... Wow! Yes, I'll make sure he knows. I'll have him phone you as soon as he gets back. Thanks. Bye."

I put the receiver back softly and stood up. "Wow," I breathed. I glanced out the window and down to Alisha's place. I could see them putting stuff into their car. They'd be up in a few minutes.

I grabbed a piece of notepaper and a pen from the kitchen drawer and scribbled:

Trevor,

Guess what? Cyril phoned to tell you that you've been chosen to fly with him to Toronto next month to observe the Canadian National Track competitions. Down the road they're thinking of placing you on a developmental team. WOW! They must really think you're something!

WAY TO GO!

Nikki

P.S. Phone him as soon as you get home.

I ran downstairs to Trevor's room and laid the note on his dresser. I stopped and chewed the end of the pen for a moment. Then I picked the note up again and folded it in half. In big letters on the outside, I wrote:

TO: THE DRAGON IN THE CLOUDS.

I propped it up where he'd be sure to see it, and ran outside to tell Mom the news.

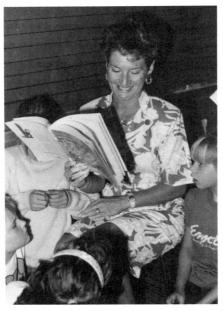

Rosemary Nelson was born in Dinsmore, Saskatchewan where her parents operated a small grain farm. Without a lot of friends to play with, her imagination became her best friend. She now lives in the Okanagan Valley in British Columbia where her acreage overlooks both the valley and lake.

Besides teaching and spending time with her family, she enjoys writing, hiking, travelling and cross country skiing.